Dear Lord, the man was in a snowbank.

She bent her knees until she crouched, pulled in a huge breath, held her arms above her head, and jumped as hard as she ever had.

Strong hands grabbed hers. He lifted her out of the hole, rolling over onto his back as she cleared the tunnel of snow he'd dug to reach the trap door, and pulled her onto himself.

They were both breathless from the exertion and lay panting for several moments.

Violet's back and feet took the brunt of the weather. She shivered, which caught the man's attention.

He sat up, holding her on his lap, and unbuttoned his shirt. Beneath the flannel he wore a red woolen undershirt, which he pulled her against as he wrapped the ends of his outer shirt around her.

"Let's get inside before we both freeze to death. I'll come back to cover this later."

Thomas stood, taking Violet in his arms and carrying her.

When she felt his large, warm hand on her skin, she learned that the nightdress that had been so lovingly created for a wedding night was torn on the back side.

And the man's hand? It was on *her* bare backside.

Praise for Sarita Leone

"A tight unpredictable plot makes *RESERVATION REQUIRED* a standout. The early 20th century—and Maine—combine to make a somewhat off the beaten path historical backdrop to this gem of a tale. A must-read for your list."

~Long and Short Reviews (4.5 Stars)

A Wylder Christmas

by

Sarita Leone

The Wylder West

A Wylder Christmas

Cover Art by *Tina Lynn Stout*

The Wild Rose Press, Inc.
PO Box 708
Adams Basin, NY 14410-0708
Visit us at www.thewildrosepress.com

Publishing History
First Cactus Rose Edition, 2020
Trade Paperback ISBN 978-1-5092-3458-5
Digital ISBN 978-1-5092-3459-2

The Wylder West
Published in the United States of America

Dedication

For Vito Leone

~

Ten Christmases later and I still miss him
every single day…because love never dies.

Chapter 1

December 1878

Life changes in a heartbeat.

One instant Violet plodded through the snowstorm, bent nearly double against the onslaught of fat flakes and icy pellets borne on a brutal wind.

Then, a heartbeat.

And in the next, she lay flat on her back, staring up into the purplish gray sky.

Dawn hadn't arrived yet, which suited her. No doubt the day would prove to be gloomy, and the purple hues were surely far more attractive than whatever would follow.

Which she would witness from her indelicate position unless she formulated a way to regain her feet.

Reaching the schoolhouse early to prepare for the upcoming Christmas party should have been uncomplicated. A short walk through the snow, and a few quiet hours to work on decorations. She wanted to show her competence so Wylder would see their new schoolteacher cared enough to work diligently to make their holiday gathering successful.

At present, the only ability she demonstrated was clumsiness. Lord, she hoped no one saw her tumble!

She rolled to her right side and kicked at the tangle of fabric around her ankles. The woolen scarf her sister had knitted for her—now a soggy mess—nearly strangled her so she tugged it out from beneath her shoulder and put one hand down. She'd landed in a snowbank, so her arm sank in up to her elbow. When she pulled it back, snow remained between her coat and shirtwaist sleeve. At this point it was not her biggest challenge.

This must be how a turtle feels when it's tipped over.

Violet wiggled to the left, then to the right, and rocked herself back and forth until she tilted to one side far enough that she managed to sit upright. Again, she untangled her skirt from her legs. She dug her boots into the snow and leaned forward to rise halfway before her heel slipped on the ice and she fell face first into the white mound beside her.

At least now she wasn't on her back.

Colder and wetter than ever, she had little hope of getting up.

Footsteps crunched in the snow near her head.

Strong hands grabbed her upper arms and pulled her out of the snow. She was turned and lifted by someone who smelled of wood smoke and pipe tobacco.

Liberation from her misery came in the span of a heartbeat or two—maybe three, at most. She wiped a gloved hand across her eyes, clearing the snow from her face so she could see.

Her heart skipped a beat when she gazed at the chiseled chin of the man who held her. He looked down with concern in his eyes.

"Can you stand on your own?" Warm breath fanned her cheek. Cradled in his embrace, she nearly forgot her unfortunate state of affairs: on a deserted, dark street, soaking wet and defenseless, with a stranger. "Let's get you out of this snowbank and we'll test those legs."

"That would be nice, thank you."

He carried her until they were clear of the icy patch that had laid her low and then stomped out a small circle to give her a place to stand. She instantly missed the warmth and security of his arms when he put her down.

"How does that feel?" He kept a hand on her shoulder. "Legs all right? Everything else? You took quite a tumble. And not once, but twice."

She didn't need to be reminded that she'd flopped around in the snow like a graceless seal. And this man had apparently witnessed the entire spectacle.

If she weren't so miserable, she would be embarrassed.

That would come later. Now, her teeth began to chatter.

"I'm f-fine, t-thank you." She wanted to say more, to show her gratitude, but speaking didn't come easy.

"You're not as fine as you think you are. You're probably soaked to the skin, and near frozen. Wait here while I fetch your things."

Her things? Her mind refused to work properly. She watched as he turned and headed back to the pile of snow that had been her temporary prison. He leaned down, stuck an arm into the snowbank, and pulled something out. When he shook it, she recognized her book bag. It had been a going-away gift from her sister Pansy.

A length of red ribbon that would look lovely

draped above the schoolhouse door trailed from it like an icy tail.

The bag didn't interest her as much as the man did. Tall, with a broad back and long legs that clambered over snowdrifts as if they were anthills, his rugged good looks appealed, even in the darkness. He wore a thick brown coat and a wide-brimmed hat. He had dark hair, although in the pre-dawn snowy gloom she could be mistaking brown for black. Whatever it was, glistening strands peeked out above his coat collar.

He pulled one of her gloves from the patch of ice that had dumped her onto her face. She hadn't realized she'd lost it until she saw the scrap of wool dangling from his fingertip like a tiny, black spot against a field of white.

He returned to her side but didn't offer the possessions. He tucked her back in the crook of one arm and placed the other arm around her shoulders. Of course, had the circumstances been different, she would have balked at the impropriety. Instead she leaned against him, grateful for the warmth and shelter of his form.

"We need to get you inside. The schoolhouse is close. Do you think you can walk? I can carry you if need be."

Tempting.

But out of the question. She was not some fainting female who required rescuing.

Indignation sent a hot spark up her spine so she straightened, shook her head, and said, "No, thank you. I am perfectly f-f-fi—I a-am—" Her teeth nipped the end of her tongue. Violet raised a hand and covered her mouth. "Oh!"

4

His gaze was sharp. "You are freezing."

She stared into his eyes but didn't comprehend his meaning. Freezing? Yes, she had been cold, but the sensation lessened with each breath. Everything about her grew dim, including the snow. Her heartbeat slowed. Snowflakes blended into a white blanket, one she no longer feared falling into.

Violet met the stranger's gaze. His eyes, like his hair, were dark. They might be the perfect place to drown if she were ever in a position to swim again.

Although right now, settling into the snowy drape closing them off from the rest of the world seemed the best option as her heart stuttered and breathing became a hardship.

"Stay with me. Don't go to sleep, stay with me. Damn, but we've got to get you warm."

He tore open his coat. A button flew off into the snow. Inside the garment, a soft fur lining over deep blue flannel covered the man's broad chest.

The stranger lifted her into his arms again, pulled her close against his body, and wrapped his coat around her. Then he strode through the snowstorm. Violet wondered if this is what it felt like to fly.

He tightened his grip on her, sending her face flush against his chest. Dry, warm fabric brushed her skin.

His heart beat a steady cadence beside her cheek. Then the world, with its swirling whiteness, suddenly went black—and Violet welcomed the darkness.

Chapter 2

Violet opened her eyes and blinked.

The last time she had been lying on her back she'd been staring up into the dark sky with snow and ice daggers falling on her. Now, there were no cold pellets, biting breezes, or ominous clouds but the expanse above showed an unfamiliar shade of ecru.

Where in heaven could she be?

Then it hit her. Maybe this *was* Heaven.

But if she were dead, where were the angels? Saint Peter? God?

Where was Jasper? Surely if she had died and gone to the hereafter, her betrothed would meet her and welcome her in, wouldn't he? Granted, they had scarcely known each other before she agreed to the engagement but still—wouldn't he be obligated to greet her when she arrived in paradise? Surely, he would.

Unless she wasn't in Heaven.

Perhaps she had taken a detour.

After all, she had agreed to marry Jasper Abraham under false pretenses. That must be a solid strike against her.

And there had been all those times she had had jealous thoughts regarding her eldest sister. It wouldn't matter to God that Lily took pleasure in bragging to the rest of her siblings about her social popularity, witty conversational skills, or favor with Father and Mother.

No, God would not think jealousy warranted, under any circumstances. Another strike—or several if one counted each individual instance—then.

Duly noted in the Book of Good and Evil (because there surely must be one—otherwise how could their actions ever be tallied?) there were dozens of minor-but-still-less-than-kind acts or uncharitable opinions listed against her. How many damning red marks would there be? No way for a mortal to know.

Not even if they were no longer mortal.

That was it, then. She must be dead.

Violet pushed herself to a sitting position, noting as she did that beds in the afterlife were soft and quilts warm.

Her heart faltered in her chest. Of course, they were.

Everything here was warm!

She looked down at herself. She wasn't a specter or an unseemly swath of fog. Her mortal form had accompanied her on her journey. Gratitude swept over her. It would not do to float about in an undignified cloud, as she had always imagined heavenly beings must do.

But she wasn't in Heaven.

A bead of perspiration slid from beneath the hair at the nape of her neck and traveled down her spine. Perhaps cloud beings were not sturdy enough for whatever awaited them in this place. They might need solid forms to perform their duties—the duties that would be theirs for eternity.

She had never shoveled coal before. Not on a significant scale, anyhow. Scoops from coal shuttle to fireplace mustn't count as actual coal shoveling—at least she didn't think it would. Seven lumps on a metal scoop could not be the same as shoveling for Satan.

Violet ran a shaky hand down the front of her form from collarbone to middle. The neat white shirtwaist was gone. She swished her legs about beneath the quilt. They were unencumbered, no heavy woolen stockings or skirt layers to impede movement.

She shouldn't be dead. How could she be dead when she was charged with planning the town's biggest winter event? The Christmas party wasn't going to happen at all now, not with her demise. Disappointing everyone by depriving them of holiday fun must add marks against her in the Book of Good and Evil. Maybe those were the marks that sent her to Hell.

How many people lived in Wylder? Whatever the tally, if each resident's disappointment counted against her, that would surely tip the scales in favor of her receiving a shovel instead of angel wings.

She tried moistening her lips, but her tongue was hot and dry, and stuck to the lower corner of her mouth.

She blinked. She *should* be crying, for goodness sake! But there were no tears from her burning eyes.

Her mind scrambled to discern the truth, but her skin was oh, so hot.

She remembered being cold. Horribly frozen. Icier than she had ever been—and unable to feel most of her body while her mind faded into nothingness.

It was death, that nothingness.

She was dead.

A sudden wave of heat crashed over her. She closed her eyes and groaned.

"I'm in Hell!"

She turned her head toward the sound of an

opening door. It was almost impossible to focus with eyes that felt filled with sand.

A form entered and moved to the foot of the bed. She blinked, wondering what tomfoolery this was. Minions were supposed to be horned and hooved, not tall and handsome!

"Are you the devil?" A whisper. She fell back against the bedding when it became too exhausting to remain upright.

The man placed a tray on the bedside table. He bent over her, and a vaguely familiar scent swept up her nostrils and into her too-hot head.

"I've been called a lot of things, but this is a first."

She closed her eyes to avoid the searing pain. "Satan?"

"Not today, ma'am."

Chapter 3

Gentle fingers swept across her forehead, then down over her temples, and finally to her throat. They pressed, and twin twinges of pain got her attention.

Violet opened her eyes. Brightness made her snap them closed.

"Draw the curtain, please. The lady's eyes aren't accustomed to sunlight yet," directed a male voice. "Let's see if we can't make her shift back to civilization a smooth one."

She sensed movement around her. A straightening of the bedding. A creaking floorboard.

"Now, why don't you try that again. Can you open your eyes for us?"

Cautiously she opened one, then the other.

A man stood beside the bed. The doctor. She'd seen him around town.

He had shoulder length dark hair and piercing green eyes. A beard sprinkled with a bit of gray. Now, his gaze pinned hers, and she wriggled under the scrutiny.

She raised a hand to her head to discover her hair lay across the pillow, out of its typical bun. She had no memory of undoing it.

She had no consistent recollections at all. Disjointed wisps of memory floated through her mind. Were they real? Or had she been dreaming?

"Good. I've been keeping an eye on you since you've been here."

She wondered how long she'd been here, wherever here was. She didn't have time to ask. He seemed full of questions.

"Do you know your name?"

What an amusing man. Of course she knew her own name!

Violet nodded. "I do." She tried to clear her throat, but it felt as if someone had stuffed a straw bale down past her molars.

He reached across the bed and took a glass from the woman standing there. He bent and brought it to Violet's lips.

"Small mouthfuls, now. Just enough to wet your whistle so we can have a little chat. Then I'll leave you to rest." When she had taken a few sips—which slid down her throat and soothed the uncomfortable spots—he handed the glass back to the woman. "Now, you know your name. Would you mind sharing that news with me?"

"Violet. My name is Violet Mae Bloom."

The man's eyebrows went up. His lips twitched but he didn't laugh.

If her head didn't feel so muddled, she would have left the middle name out of the recitation. The family joke that she—and her sisters, as well—hated, but one that her father loved, could be embarrassing. They adored him and endured the matching middle name he'd given to each of his daughters but enduring a thing was worlds away from liking it.

"Miss Bloom, do you know who I am?"

"You're Doctor Sullivan. I've seen you...ah, well,

I've seen you around town now and again."

The truth was, she'd seen the doctor entering and exiting the Wylder County Social Club which, despite its high-falootin' name, was a whorehouse. Violet had been a resident of Wylder for eight months, but she'd learned the truth of the place in the first eight minutes.

Well, that was an exaggeration. It took a bit longer than that.

But the local ladies had warned her the week she had arrived to steer clear of Miss Adelaide and her "girls" if she wanted to keep her reputation intact.

"Very good. I admit, I've seen you about town, as well. I should make more effort to meet people as they get here but, in my defense, my days are full, and those niceties sometimes slip by me."

She imagined his life must be full, what with all the coming and going she had seen. It wasn't her nature to spy on others but the vantage point from the school yard gave an almost-unobstructed view of the Five Star Saloon. Well, sort of unobstructed if she walked to the furthest edge of the school yard and across the front church yard and then leaned over a bit. A big, neck-stretching bit.

The Social Club was tucked discreetly beyond the telegraph office, on the other side of the railroad tracks. It was a short walk down Old Cheyenne Road. Unless a man was headed to send a telegraph, if he sauntered down that way there was a real good chance he was headed to the Wylder County Social Club.

The doctor looked reputable, and his profession made him somewhat scholarly, but from the frequency of his visits to Miss Adelaide and her girls, he must have a powerful, ah, vitality about him.

She hadn't seen him frequenting the area of the Social Club lately. Not since he wed, actually.

Eliza Jane O'Hanlan had been a prickly sort of spinster but since she and Doc married her demeanor was less starched. Apparently being newlywed agreed with her. Who could tell? Violet suspected that Eliza Jane's husband smoothed her pricklier bits with all that vitality.

Doc Sullivan stroked his beard with quiet regard.

Violet colored when he tapped the pistol on his hip because it forced her to do a thing she tried to avoid: She dropped her gaze. Mother had taught her a lady kept her gaze above a man's belt at all time. All times, mind you!

Then, she remembered Christmas. Parties didn't plan themselves—and if she weren't dead, she had to get to it!

"I need to go. Christmas grows closer and I need to leave, please."

When she tried to move toward the side of the bed, the doctor put a hand on her shoulder and held her back. She pressed against his hand before she realized that he had an unyielding grip. Defeated, she settled against the pillow behind her.

"Not so fast. Christmas will wait, I'm sure."

Violet sighed. He had no idea how much she needed to do—and none of it would get done while she lay about like a popinjay with nowhere to go.

"I hope I'm not out of line, but I hear a beautiful southern lilt to your voice, and it tugs on my heartstrings. If you would indulge me by telling me where you're from I'd be grateful."

She pushed a hand on the mattress. When he

discerned she intended to sit up, he motioned to the woman standing nearby. They each put a hand beneath her arms and helped her slide toward the headboard. The woman arranged the pillows while Violet pulled the blankets up to her armpits.

"I'm from Charleston, South Carolina. My family is still there."

Doctor Sullivan pulled a straight-back wooden chair up beside the bed and sat down. He nodded appreciatively. "I thought as much. I've been out here for a while, but I can still hear a southern belle from a mile away. Tell me, if you don't mind, a little about your family."

The question seemed odd so she considered her reply.

"My parents and three sisters live in Charleston, in the home we have always lived in. My father is a lawyer. None of my sisters is yet wed, so they all help Mother with her charitable causes."

They were the barest facts about a family so complicated it would take days to explain them to this man.

"Have you no brothers?"

An innocent question, but it brought a sharp pain to the center of her chest. Memories weren't all sunshine and laughter for anyone, but especially not for those whose families had served in the war.

"We lost my brother at Chancellorsville."

"I'm so sorry to hear that. It was a victory for our side against the Union, but at a dear cost. War is like that, I'm afraid." He patted her hand. "Was your father there, as well?"

"Yes. He managed to bring my brother's body

home. Mother appreciated that. I believe she would have been crushed if she hadn't been able to lay Stuart to rest in the family plot. Did you serve, Doctor?"

He nodded. "I did."

"I thought perhaps you had."

"I stood shoulder to shoulder with my Confederate brothers, as your kin did. They said it was a rich man's war and a poor man's fight, but we know better. The cost was greater than any money could ever account for."

A knock came at the door. The woman, who had yet to introduce herself, opened it and allowed the caller to enter. He appeared familiar but Violet couldn't quite place him until he spoke.

"Well, this is good news, indeed. You're awake and looking better than you have in days."

She instantly recalled the deep masculine voice. The stranger who rescued her when she had fallen in the snowbank!

Chapter 4

Doctor Sullivan said she could get out of bed and walk about the room if she felt up to it. But he opposed her leaving while she was still, in his words, "gaining her wits back."

It was aggravating to be trapped in a stranger's home. And it was improper for a maiden woman to be sleeping beneath a man's roof. But her efforts to sway the physician were in vain. He'd insisted and she had no choice but to comply.

Gertie, the neighbor woman who had assisted the doctor, remained behind to help while she bathed and changed into a fresh nightdress. When Violet slipped her arms into the garment held out for her, she recognized it as one of her own. The decorative stitching on the white cuffs had been embroidered by her sister Pansy. It was one of her contributions to Violet's trousseau.

It had been intended for her wedding night.

Violet had never worn it.

"How did my nightdress get here?" Her fingers were unusually clumsy, her hands trembled, and the exertion of the simple toilette had her knees shaking. Once buttoned up, she sat in a chair beside the window while the other woman gathered the garments she'd removed. "It was at my home when I saw it last."

The older woman tied the towel around the

nightclothes and left the bundle beside the door. She turned the used water into the philodendron on a side table, wiped the basin with a rag, and returned it to the washstand.

"When Coyote saw your state and said you couldn't be moved, Thomas went to your place and got some things. Good that he did, too. We wouldn't want you to be cold now, would we?"

Gertie reminded Violet of the Widow Smithers from back home in Charleston. Their closest neighbor had the same soft way about her. She had work-worn hands and a sad air that draped like a shawl across her shoulders. Missus Smithers lost her husband and two sons at Chancellorsville. Violet's father had returned them home to her on the same trip he'd made with his own son.

The widow had reason to be melancholy forever after. Violet wondered what had happened to Gertie to make her that way, as well.

Her mind must still be chilled. She understood half of what was being said. Despite not wanting to appear dull-witted, she asked, "Whoever is Coyote? And Thomas?"

Too tired to attempt it herself, she allowed her hair to be brushed. The rhythmic tug and pull of the brush through her locks quieted her muddled mind.

"Why, I keep forgetting you're new around here. You really haven't had the chance to meet many of us, have you, what with the sadness that you found at your doorstep." The other woman's touch was gentle. There were some snarls, from being abed for a spell, but she coaxed them out without tugging at Violet's scalp. "That must have been an awful shock for you. We were all sorry for your situation, but it's not our way to impose at such times. But we're here if you need anything, remember that. And you'll surely meet everyone at the Christmas party in the schoolhouse. We're all looking forward to it."

Violet swallowed around the tightness in her throat. She didn't deserve this woman's compassion. If she knew the truth about the betrothal or her feelings for Jasper, she wouldn't think much of her at all.

"I am grateful for your kindness." She ran a hand across her eyes and took a deep breath. "But I'm still confused about the people you mentioned."

"Sorry, I am distracted by your hair. It's so thick and soft." She handed the brush over Violet's shoulder and began to braid. "Most people call the doc Coyote. Don't ask me why because I don't know and, between us, I'm not sure I want to know. Men should have their secrets, same as we do. And Thomas? Why, this is his house you're staying in. He's the one who found you buried in a snowbank. You're lucky to be alive. If Thomas hadn't spotted you, you would've frozen to death."

Violet took a deep breath as tears gathered in the corners of her eyes. She had a hazy recollection of the events of that morning.

A powerful man emerged from a snowstorm, picked her up when she was so cold she thought she would shatter into a million pieces, and carried her, snugged against his hard, warm body, to safety while she fell into a dreamy slumber.

Gertie spoke the truth.

Violet owed the man her life.

Chapter 5

Gertie assured Violet she would return the following day to check on her.

Finally alone, she had a chance to consider her surroundings.

The room was well-decorated and comfortable, with pale green walls and matching window dressings. The four carved columns on the poster bed, its headboard, and footboard were intricate and beautiful. The wood shone, and it was obvious that someone had gone to some effort to craft such a fine piece of furniture. The side tables, as well as the fireplace mantel, matched the bed. All exquisite, and more like what she had grown up with back east than what she expected to see in the wild west.

A built-in bookcase held several leather-bound volumes. Giving in to her piqued curiosity, she walked barefoot to the case and perused the titles.

They were impressive. Shakespeare stood beside Walt Whitman, Herman Melville, and Ralph Waldo Emerson, to name a few. Some of the works she had in her own small library, but others drew her teacher's heart to full attention.

She selected a slim volume of poetry and walked back to the chair beside the window. A sufficient amount of stuffing made for a comfortable seat so she settled in, tucked her legs up under her, and began to read.

One loses track of time when immersed in a good book, so she had no idea how many hours passed before she heard a knock on the door.

"Miss Bloom? May I come in?"

Violet gathered her shawl close around her shoulders and called, "Yes, of course you may."

The door swung in and a wooden, towel-covered tray entered. Then, the man carrying it followed, and the room felt smaller than it had seconds earlier.

"I hoped you were awake. How are you feeling?"

He pulled a side table over until it stood beside her chair. He'd brought tea—the big lump beneath the towel gave the teapot's presence away. Something sweet, too, if she could trust her nose.

"Fine, thank you. I feel quite silly imposing upon you this way. It appears that I've been a rather large nuisance already. I assure you, I'm well enough to return home."

He picked up the wooden chair that stood near the bed and brought it over. He set it down and sat in it, smiling as he did so. "That's not what our town's best—and only—doctor has to say about it. No, he made it clear: You're to spend the night where you are."

"I'm sorry." She tucked her hands into the folds of the floral-patterned quilt that lay across her lap. "I'm sure you don't need a stranger in your house."

Removing the towel from the tray and laying it to the side, he shook his head.

"We're a small town. There are no strangers here in Wylder, only folks we haven't yet met."

"You're very nice."

He met her gaze and shook his head a second time. A black curl dropped over one side of his forehead. He tucked the strand back out of the way and said, "I'm not that nice, believe me. But since we haven't been formally introduced and it's too late now to wait for a social occasion to have that happen, I'm Thomas Harvey."

The smile he offered with the name made the room brighter. Besides being brave and accommodating to half-dead strangers, he had had a magnetic appeal.

She'd landed in a fairy tale. The problem with fairy tales? Heroines should be qualified to assume the role, which she was not.

But he didn't know that, so she returned his smile and introduced herself. "I'm Violet Bloom, the schoolteacher here in town. I think this might be overdue, but thank you for saving me the way you did. I owe you my life."

He drew in a sudden sharp breath and looked down to the tea tray. After a moment, he raised his gaze. "Life's too precious to hand over that easily. I'm glad I saw you when I did. You're the only schoolteacher this town has, and we'd be lost if we let anything happen to you."

"The only, so the best? Like the doctor?" She teased, hoping to see the sparkle that had left his eyes when she'd spoken about owing him return.

His dark brown eyes shone as he raised an eyebrow. "Why yes, of course you're the best. You should know that already. May I pour you a cup of tea before it gets cold?" He began to pour without waiting for a reply. "Would you like a tea cake or a biscuit? I must confess, I did not make either but they both smell mighty good."

When he reached over to set her teacup on the edge of the table, she caught the same whiff of masculine deliciousness he'd swept over her the other morning in the snow.

Something smelled mighty good, indeed.

Chapter 6

Her host insisted Violet rest after tea. She resisted—but ever-so slightly.

Bone-deep weariness consumed her. All fingers and toes were where they should be, but they pained her. Tenderness in her chest and throat, reminders of the frigid air that had entered her lungs, made breathing a chore.

When he left with the tea tray and closed the door behind him, she removed her bed jacket and shawl, laid them across the foot of the bed, and crawled into the inviting nest of feather tick flannel.

Her mind fell into slumber almost before her eyelids dropped.

Sleep was often an elusive bedfellow for Violet. She was a night walker, prone to being awake and restless when others slept. That's what had brought her out before daylight the morning she fell. She simply could not sleep so decided to work in the schoolroom instead.

But now she dozed without effort, a dreamless, restful slumber that her soul desperately needed for rejuvenation.

When she woke shadows had crept into the room. She rose and walked to the window.

Outside, swaths of purple, lavender, and deep blue slashed the sky. Snow had stopped falling and shadows sent purplish casts onto the drifts that lined the street below.

The house stood in a residential area of town she hadn't been in before. Rows of houses were built back from the broad street. She saw one red brick home and wondered who could afford such an indulgence.

The nearest had trees planted in their yards. All branches were leafless now, but she imagined it would look inviting come spring.

Her own residence was tiny by comparison to these. Even with the heavy snow covering she could tell she had a much smaller yard. Although she did have two trees near her back door, which delighted her.

The modest structure was adequate for her needs. As she didn't see her circumstances changing in the foreseeable future, it would remain so. Owning a home was more than many other unmarried twenty-two-year-old women could claim.

It had come to her with little effort and no financial investment. As were so many things that had taken place in the past year, it came as a complete surprise.

Jasper Abraham pledged he had a home she would be mistress of, and that it would be hers for as long as she wanted. She believed him—but she had also assumed they would be sharing the house. That turned out to not be the case at all.

When she arrived, she laid claim to the place. The legal move had not been complicated since Jasper had been kind enough to leave a letter naming her its owner in his absence.

So, she had a home. Not as grand as this one, but gratitude for the small dwelling, and the man who left it to her, filled her right down to her soul. Without it, a return to Charleston in defeat would have been unavoidable. She would have disappointed the family—and they had already endured enough hardship.

No, she was going to stay in Wylder despite the true circumstances of her life. Moving out west was her second chance, a way to put the past to rest and start over. She wasn't going to admit defeat, whatever happened.

This brush with death gave her another reason to begin again. She could be deceased at this very moment, instead of surrounded by comfort, safe and well-cared for, and contemplating how to make this move west successful. Like a cat with nine lives, ready to embrace change at every turn, she intended to make this next chapter of her life meaningful.

A cat!

Oh, good heavens!

Violet had to go home—and now. She turned from the window as she pulled the hem of her nightdress upward. The buttons were still fastened, but she tugged hard enough that something tore. There was room to pull the garment overhead and off her shoulders, but she knocked into the side table when she wrestled with the fabric. The book of poetry thudded to the floor, but she was powerless to retrieve it—not that she would have, right then—because the cuffs of the nightdress were buttoned and her arms were trapped. She found herself a prisoner in a garment fashioned to please a husband she'd never met, stark naked, hands pinned in the sleeves, and without any idea how to get out of the predicament.

A sharp rapping sounded at the door seconds before it opened into the room.

She pulled her hands high, covering her breasts and, hopefully, most of the rest of her from view. Her shoulders and backside were bare.

"I heard something fall! Are you—" The expression on Thomas Harvey's face hid nothing. Shock showed in his eyes, his brows went so high on his head they practically hit his hairline, and his jaw dropped. His mouth snapped shut—and his gaze raked her figure the way one who comes upon an unexpected scene reacts before remembering their manners.

His lips curved upward at the corners.

Violet bent her knees and crouched behind the wonderfully overstuffed—and amply wide—chair. "I need to go."

He cleared his throat. "But you heard the doc. You must remain at least one more night. You are no trouble, I assure you. In fact, I have arranged for a hearty dinner, in an effort to bolster your constitution."

Every minute counted. "That's all quite nice and I assure you, I am in your debt, but I need to leave. I cannot delay so if you would please go so I may dress, I will be on my way."

She peeked around the side of the chair, wishing he would close the door. A cool breeze hit a rather delicate area of her anatomy.

"I cannot keep you captive in my home so if you wish to go, I won't try to stop you." He cleared his throat a second time, and now he chuckled. "Although I have to say that my ever-so-brief glimpse of your current situation shows that you are trapped by your own nightdress. Would you like some help getting free of it?"

Tossing herself backward out the window and

running home barefoot and bare-assed almost felt like the best option. Humiliation swept over her in a hot wave followed by an even warmer wash of scorching indignation. How dare he laugh at her predicament?

"No, I do not require your help. If you would be so kind—please, leave. I need to go home now. I don't have a moment to lose!"

The floorboards creaked as he took a step into the hall and began to pull the door closed.

She started to stand but when the door didn't close fully, she paused. The half-crouch didn't feel as comfortable as the full had been, but her anatomy was out of the breeze so there was that.

"May I ask why you're so all-fired ready to go home now? Did I offend you in some way?"

She sighed. It wasn't his fault that she'd been caught in this position.

"No, nothing of the sort. I have a cat at home I can't neglect one minute more. I should have remembered her the instant my eyes opened, yet I've been here all day and this is the first thought I've given to the animal. I need to go home and tend her—you must see that, don't you?"

Violet waited for what felt like forever for the man to leave.

"Your cat is a sweet little orange thing that likes to pounce on feathers and makes a sloppy mess when she drinks milk. She is fine, I promise."

She stood, forgetting about her dilemma. "How do you know that?"

He glanced back at her, and this time his gaze remained on her face. "I found the cat when I went to fetch your essentials. It's not been neglected so you don't need to fret. Now, I think you should get yourself untangled and lie down. Your cheeks are flushed from your exertion. Coyote would be madder than a hornet if he knew I'd let you get so riled. Take it from me, you don't want to see him in an ornery mood, so for both our sakes, please get back in bed."

He turned and walked out, pulling the door closed behind him.

Violet hitched a breath. Now she not only owed him for her life, but Ginny's as well.

Her debt to Thomas Harvey grew steeper with each passing hour and she had no idea how she would ever satisfy the man.

Chapter 7

Violet contemplated climbing out of the window and vanishing into the night. She might have tried to do so but she still did not know what street this house occupied or where it was in relation to her own. No familiar landmarks in sight to give hints about her location presented a puzzle without any means of solving it.

After she had gotten back into her nightdress and bed jacket, she gathered her shawl about her shoulders and settled into the big chair. Exhaustion claimed her. It was somewhat alarming that she should tire so easily. Hopefully, it would be a short-lived condition. She had too many duties to be laid low for an extended period.

Schools in the Wyoming territory went by the legislative mandate of 1873 that made attendance for children ages seven through sixteen compulsory for three months of each calendar year. Since most ranchers, homesteaders, and farmers relied on child labor to run their operations during the spring, summer, and fall months, schools filled during the unproductive winter season.

The Wylder School saw its greatest number of pupils in these cold months. Closing for a day or even a week due to inclement weather could not be avoided but keeping the doors closed because she felt too poorly to teach would not do. She had to regain her strength—

and soon.

The chair provided the ideal spot for rumination, so she let her mind wander. There were pressing matters to decide regarding her pupils, so she considered her options. Implementing the mandate proved difficult. For some families, sending children to town, whatever the season, was impractical. Any family that lived further than four or five miles from the schoolhouse considered the day a waste because of time lost on the long walk to and from town. If a buckboard became available with an older child to drive it, families often shared transport. Otherwise, pupils remained at home.

Many families still considered education frivolous. Changing that way of thinking turned out to be tough, if not impossible.

Violet had been cautioned that teaching school in the territory would be a challenge. She'd heard stories from teachers who had tried it, failed, and returned east. There were also warnings from educators on the futility of attempting to sway the wild west way of thinking. Better, they advised, to teach to an empty schoolroom than tangle with locals.

She didn't agree with either of those views. Children needed an education—period.

Her duties included seeing that as many as possible received schooling, whatever the cost and however she had to accomplish it.

An aching head forced her to close her eyes, tuck her feet up on the chair beneath her, and rest a temple against the upholstery. In a heartbeat, Violet was asleep.

It wasn't a refreshing rest but rather one of those light intervals between wakefulness and deep sleep that leaves one more tired than ever. Vivid, sometimes frightening, dreams punctuated her nap. Visions of lathered wild horses chasing her, their hooves clattering against ice-covered ground, sent vibrations deep into her soul. Darkness surrounded her and voices called her name.

Her earliest thought when she woke came from the dream she'd just had. Someone called to her, a bang punctuating each syllable.

Vi—bang! O—bang! Let—bang!

She opened her eyes to silence. No shouting. No pounding. Barely the sound of a log sputtering in the fireplace.

She stretched. Glancing over her shoulder, through the window she saw that night had fallen. Good. The sooner these hours passed, the quicker she could return home, to the place where the only one who saw her in an indelicate position was her dear, sweet kitty.

When she thought the evening would slip away without incident, a knock on the bedroom door dropped her heart to her toes. It could only be one person—the man she most adamantly did not wish to see.

Still, she was a guest in his home.

And he'd saved her life.

And Ginny's.

"Yes?"

"I have your dinner. May I come in?"

To his credit, he did not touch the doorknob. She watched it for signs of motion but there were none.

She wondered if there were still time to climb out the window.

"Miss Bloom? Your dinner?"

He would surely enter if she did not reply so she

called out, "Thank you, but I am not hungry. Good night."

Silence.

That had been easy!

There was another knock on the door.

Maybe it wasn't as easy as that.

"Now listen, you need to eat to regain your strength. Coyote—Doctor Sullivan left instructions that you were to be rested, nourished, and kept calm. I implore you, eat your meal so you recover."

Violet regarded obstinacy as a character trait socially unacceptable for anything other than mules. In humans it appeared childish and unflattering.

But she dug her heels in anyway.

"No, thank you."

She heard him lean against the doorframe. And then, a sigh that was loud enough to reach her.

A voice inside her head urged her to relent.

But a second voice insisted she was too mortified to face the man. What if he chose to dine with her? What then? She couldn't very well chase him from the room—he had every right to eat in any room of his own house if he chose to do so.

What a fine spot she had landed herself in this time.

"Miss Bloom, I apologize for earlier. I didn't mean to embarrass you—and I assure you I am as shocked as you are. But we are adults and should be able to put that aside, so why don't you consent to eat this substantial meal that Gertie has prepared for you? Please?"

She swallowed. No man other than Father or Stuart had ever spoken with such compassion, nor had touched her heart the way he did. She should concede, she knew that as well as she knew her own name.

But mortification ran deep, a close second to shame. Her shame was so ingrained that she could not put it aside.

She wanted to but could not.

Her voice hitched when she replied. "T-thank you and Gertie both, but I cannot eat tonight. I am going to retire now. Good night, Mister Harvey."

A second loud sigh came from beyond the door.

"Good night, Miss Bloom."

Chapter 8

Sleep did not come swiftly.

Violet tossed and turned, pulling the floral quilt up beneath her chin to ward off a chill, and then pushing it down to her waist in a fit of heat. Her constitution betrayed her, turning from icy to boiling in turn, leaving her no room for ease between its fits.

It was her due, she supposed. Her punishment for being so vile to the gentleman who sheltered her. She had behaved dreadfully, and it made her furious with herself.

Her bouts of bad humor could not be contained despite her most valiant attempts to do so.

Thomas Harvey. His name was as solid as his nature. He had saved her, brought her to his home, cared for her, tended to her and her cat, and she had behaved like an ill-humored child.

Certainly, it was unbecoming of an unmarried woman to expose herself to a man the way she had, but it had been an accident. And, as he pointed out, they were adults.

Or at least he acted like an adult. She, however, had not.

She rolled over and buried her face in the pillow. Praying did not come without effort for her but perhaps if she prayed to vanish before morning, God would take pity on her tortured soul and allow her this one wish.

But if she disappeared there was no chance of seeing Mister Harvey ever again.

And she rather enjoyed the man.

What was a single woman to do, out here in the west where the niceties of South Carolina society were nonexistent?

The only way she intended to go back to Charleston included a pine box. If the place didn't kill her, she planned to make this work.

The very last notion Violet had as sleep finally, mercifully, claimed her included visions of happy schoolchildren.

How much time elapsed between her silent resolution to remain in Wylder and the loud shouts and insistent shaking that woke her she did not know.

"Wake up!"

Thomas Harvey's hands gripped her upper arms, his face inches from her own when she opened her eyes.

"Miss Bloom—Violet, can you hear me? You need to get up—now."

She jumped as a crash sounded beyond the closed window.

"What's happening?" He helped her out of bed and onto her feet. She reached for her shawl, groping in the darkness at the foot of the bed but he grabbed her hand.

"No time for that. Come on, you've got to hide."

Glass shattered. Loud, unintelligible shouts met their ears.

He half-dragged her around the big bed and into the far corner of the room. An ornately carved tri-fold wooden screen occupied the space. He pushed it aside and pulled her behind it with him.

"Listen, you need to stay as quiet as you can. No matter what you hear, no matter what it sounds like, do not make any noise."

He ran a hand over the woodwork in the corner as more tinkling glass and yelling reached them. Violet threw herself against him when something crashed in the yard. Solid muscles rippled beneath his garments as his fingertips pressed a latch and a wooden panel swung into the room.

"You'll be safe in here." He removed her arms from around his shoulders and took one of her hands in his. He ran her fingers over a spot inside the secret compartment. "When I close this panel, I want you to hit this button. The lock will fasten from the inside. Lock it—and no one will be able to get to you."

He lifted her and placed her on a shelf beyond the panel. A tiny space, it afforded her room to kneel with its interior ceiling brushing the top of her head.

More mayhem from the street and yards.

"Do you understand how to lock this?"

She was too frightened to speak so she nodded.

"Show me." He grabbed her hand and put her fingers on the spot. "Right there, do you feel it? Violet—do you feel the button?"

"I do—what's going on, Thomas? What is happ—"

"The sheriff expected this. We were warned, and we're ready. A mob of disgruntled ranch hands rode into town. They're liquored up and looking for trouble. Don't you worry about it. Stay put. Lock yourself in and you'll be fine. Give me your word that whatever happens you won't open this panel. Not for anyone!"

Hollering and what sounded like a stampede filled the space between them. How could such a ruckus penetrate the walls of a building this way?

Fear gripped her heart. What if they were in the house?

"Come in here! Stay safe with me!" She grabbed the front of his shirt and tried to pull him into the hiding spot. "Thomas, please!"

He uncurled her fingers from his shirt front. "I'll see you again. Now promise me you'll lock this door and stay put."

She jerked her chin toward her chest. "I promise. But why can't you—"

Glass shattered and this time there was no doubt it was one of the house windows.

Thomas pushed her inside and began to close the panel. He stopped, leaned forward, and put his mouth beside her right ear. "There's a shaft behind you. If you smell smoke, push the panel to the side and slide down the chute. You'll be safe in the cellar. Remember what I'm saying, Violet. Your life's at stake here—swear that you'll heed my words."

She nodded. "I will!"

Then he put a hand behind her head and pulled her close. His lips found hers and he kissed her none-too-gently. "Sealed with a kiss," he said as he backed away, shut the panel, and left her in absolute darkness.

Violet pushed the button beneath her fingertips and heard the panel lock.

Chapter 9

Sound was muted in the hidden cupboard.

No matter how many minutes passed, her eyes did not detect light. Had she not been conscious of her eyelids she wouldn't have been able to discern whether they were open or closed.

Violet wondered if she would run out of air. For a few moments, her mind got the best of her and her heartbeat increased. It thudded in her chest so hard that she put a finger on the locking button and nearly pressed it.

But she had promised him.

They'd sealed it with a kiss. Her first kiss—and if this night did not go well it could very well be her last.

She couldn't go back on that pact, not even with her heart beating double time and threatening to burst from her chest. Perspiration broke out on her forehead, but she removed her fingers from the release button.

She would die in here before she would go back on the vow.

Thomas had mentioned a chute in the event she smelled smoke.

Detecting smoke in the cupboard meant it had an opening for it to reach her.

She felt around the edges of the panel, starting at the top and working down both sides. No indication of a break in the woodwork and no way for smoke to penetrate the space.

Violet rested her back against the wall and sucked in a deep breath. The air was warm and stale, but adequate enough to fill her lungs, making suffocation unlikely.

She jumped as gunshots rang out above the hollering, banging, and smashing.

When the wounded returned to Charleston, Violet had been a child. Father didn't want her to witness the horror, but Mother, Lily, Pansy, and Daisy all worked at the makeshift hospital, the same as most of the other local women. It had been one of the few times her mother disagreed with her father. Mother insisted that every southern woman had a right to bear witness to the atrocities inflicted by the northern soldiers to their menfolk, and that Violet was old enough to help tend the wounded.

She gave her husband no say in the affair. Violet accompanied her mother and sisters to the hospital.

They filled her days with menial tasks meant to help ease the suffering. She went for bandages and fresh linens and carried covered pails from sickrooms outdoors. She never did peek inside the pails, afraid that their contents would be too disturbing.

Conscious of her tender years, her older sisters shielded her from the most gruesome realities. Violet heard a lot of screams and many oaths that a young woman should not hear but she did not see many bloody horrors.

But she had seen a gunshot wound. One time had left an indelible impression on her mind—and a scar on her heart that still burned raw, all these years later.

The soldier had been young, hardly older than her

own twelve years. He reclined on a stretcher on the floor, having been brought in with a large contingent of wounded men. The journey to the hospital hadn't been kind to him. Dried blood stiffened his uniform and the bandage wrapped around his thigh. A wet patch of fresh blood showed as she passed him carrying an armful of clean linens.

"Miss—help me, please."

Violet paused. He waved her over, so she went to him. He had the deepest blue eyes she had ever seen. They were the color of the Atlantic Ocean during a storm, so vibrant they were mesmerizing.

"I need a new bandage and you've got those towels…please, could you put one on my leg so I don't die? I'm afraid I'll bleed to death."

When he reached down and pulled the wet bandage away, she saw the gaping hole in his flesh. It bled freely so she pressed a white towel to it and tried not to cry.

"You're saving my life." Beneath the dirt on his face, his complexion showed gray. "My name…" It looked as if he would die before finishing, but he took a deep breath and went on. "I'm Tate Taylor, miss. I owe you my life—and I won't forget it."

The heartbreaking realization that death seemed minutes away gave her strength. This might be his last conversation. It should be sweet.

"Nice to meet you, Tate. I'm Violet Bloom."

Pain twisted his face. When he could speak, he said, "Like the flower. Miss Bloom, if I live, I'm going to find you and thank you for saving my life. It's my solemn vow."

It still hurt, thinking about Tate Taylor. She often wondered what became of him, although it was likely he hadn't made it. So many valiant southern men were lost.

Her mind was forever imprinted with the sound of the young soldier's pain, the image of black char around the edges of his wound, and the notion that a weapon ended his life.

Filtering into the tight space, the sound of gunshots pushed memories from her mind.

Men were doing battle outside. And for what? What made men kill each other this way?

She understood the War for Southern Independence and its savagery. Anyone could comprehend the necessity of wartime shooting.

But this? To shoot drunkenly and endanger innocent women and children? Or to damage property held dear to those who toiled to civilize this wilderness? It was sheer insanity.

Panic brought her heartbeat up a notch. Her little house—was it being vandalized while she sat in this cupboard? Her fingers found the hidden button once again. Perhaps she should find out.

What a foolish thought! She had no idea how to get home and even if she did, how would she make her way through the shooting and madness?

Besides, she had promised Thomas.

It felt like hours that she was locked in the cupboard but eventually the sounds of chaos died down. An occasional shout or a gunshot rang out but there wasn't continuous mayhem any longer.

She considered pressing the button and going into the house to investigate. What if Thomas needed assistance? He might be hurt—or worse.

But she had given her word to stay until he

returned. She remembered the Book of Good and Evil—had that been real or was it part of a dream? She wasn't sure but her tally on the less-than-good side was substantial. It was time to turn that around. Sticking to a vow like a decent woman might sway that book calculation.

She wanted to be decent. Not just outwardly, but inside where it counted so she stayed in silence in the dark, close space.

She heard movement in the room beyond. Perhaps Thomas had finally returned!

A crash, several thuds, and some scuffling met her ears.

Gunshots sounded like cannon fire inside the tiny cubby.

Violet squeezed her eyes closed and covered her head.

When she caught a whiff of smoke, she reached for the small panel in the back of the cupboard. She slid it to the left and felt for the chute with her trembling hands.

A wooden slide dropped away from the cupboard floor. Violet turned so her bare feet hung onto the slanted surface and when the next shot rang out, she pushed off with her hands and slid down into whatever lay at the bottom of the slope.

Chapter 10

Violet pressed her back against the rough stone wall. She had landed on a pile of burlap sacks.

Her feet were bare, and the cold dirt floor numbed her toes so she folded two bags in half and stood on them. Tearing another bag open, she fashioned a shawl. It offered a tiny measure of additional warmth and holding it closed gave her something to focus on.

There was no way to tell how long she stood there. She considered sitting but scratching and scurrying sounds changed her mind. Better to remain standing. She might be resting with a mouse but with her luck the creature would turn out to be an oversized rat.

She'd stand as long as her legs held her upright.

To pass the time, she allowed musings about the upcoming Christmas party to fill her mind. Tradition called for the community celebration to be held in the schoolhouse. Arranging the event fell to the local schoolteacher, and she intended to make it extra special.

Ladies she'd spoken with at the mercantile and around town informed her that Wylder took its holiday festivities to heart. Putting on a memorable Christmas party would earn her a favorable, long-lasting impression with townsfolk.

They acted as if she didn't reside in Wylder. If teaching their children and owning a house (well, in a manner of speaking) wasn't enough for her to be counted among the townspeople, what more did one have to do to be deemed local?

It miffed her to be considered a newcomer to town after all these months.

She would make the Christmas event spectacular. It would never be up to comparison with Charleston's grand parties, but it would show these wild westerners that she had what it took to be considered one of their own.

At least, that's what she had been planning.

But her plans had a way of not working out as, well, as planned.

Take this moment in time, for example. She had not meant to be locked in subterranean confinement with a scrabbling, scampering companion, yet here she was.

Don't think about the creature. Remember, Thomas said he would come for you.

Thomas. How rapidly they had moved from formality to familiarity. She knew almost nothing about the man, yet when she thought of him, she used his given name.

Her heart skipped a beat when she heard another scratch. She had no idea what, if anything, she could do to protect herself from a menace. She was entirely defenseless. And she hated it.

From now on, there would be no leaving the house without the Remington derringer. Father had made her promise to keep it on her person, and she had on the journey west. But she had not kept to her commitment once she reached Wylder.

Time to change her bad habit of breaking promises.

A thump from above made her drop to her knees

and cover her head with the ripped burlap bag.

Several loud scraping noises followed.

Banging, almost deafening inside the small space, had her cowering in a corner. More bumps and a few thuds. Then the sound of creaking—and a grunt.

She recognized that grunt.

Violet stood. A square of sky showed above her. The open hatch was big enough for her to squeeze through if she could reach it.

Thomas's face came into view. He reached out a hand. It dangled higher than the length of her arm.

"Give me your hand and I'll pull you out."

"I can't reach you." She looked around for something to stand on but, as she had suspected, there were only sacks in the cellar. "You're too high up, I can't reach you."

The fingers dropped a few inches. Thomas shook his head and said, "I can't lean in any further without falling into the hole with you. If that happens, we'll both be trapped. Look, you'll have to jump up and grab my hand. It's the only way."

The last time Violet had jumped, she was seven.

Fifteen years of keeping her feet on the ground had not prepared her for this moment.

But the prospect of spending eternity in a dirt cellar did not appeal, so she jumped.

And missed.

"Bend your knees. Give yourself some upward motion—spring up if you can."

"I am not a grasshopper, Mister Harvey!" Now that he was being so preposterous, she could not imagine calling him by his given name.

"I did not mean to imply that you are. I'm trying to

get you out of there. So, bend your knees and jump."

Violet tested the theory. She bent her knees but that made her hips tilt and she found herself looking at her bare feet. Surely no one could be expected to jump from this position, so she stood upright—and heard her nightdress tear. She had stepped on the hem when she tested bending her knees. When she straightened, the fabric, like her, neither jumped nor stretched. She had no idea where the garment had torn and did not care to find out.

"I don't mean to rush you but if you could hurry a bit—"

"I'm trying to make haste. You don't think I like it down here, do you?" She fisted a hand on one hip and scowled up at him. "I have never had to jump like a frog from a hole, so please bear with me."

"Fine. I'm bearing." He muttered something else that she didn't catch.

"Excuse me?"

"Nothing."

"No, it wasn't nothing. I distinctly heard you say something. What did you say?"

He closed his eyes, shook his head, and said, "I said I'm bearing. You asked me to bear with you, so I'm bearing."

"What did you say after that?" She had no idea why she pressed him.

"After that? I said I'm freezing, that's what I said. Now, would you kindly put a bit of effort into your jump so I can get you out of there and I can get us both out of this miserable snow?"

Dear Lord, the man was in a snowbank.

She bent her knees until she crouched, pulled in a

huge breath, held her arms above her head, and jumped as hard as she ever had.

Strong hands grabbed hers. He lifted her out of the hole, rolling over onto his back as she cleared the tunnel of snow he'd dug to reach the trap door, and pulled her onto himself.

They were both breathless from the exertion and lay panting for several moments.

Violet's back and feet took the brunt of the weather. She shivered, which caught the man's attention.

He sat up, holding her on his lap, and unbuttoned his shirt. Beneath the flannel he wore a red woolen undershirt, which he pulled her against as he wrapped the ends of his outer shirt around her.

"Let's get inside before we both freeze to death. I'll come back to cover this later."

Thomas stood, taking Violet in his arms and carrying her.

When she felt his large, warm hand on her skin, she learned that the nightdress that had been so lovingly created for a wedding night was torn on the back side.

And the man's hand? It was on *her* bare backside.

Chapter 11

For a woman who had never been in a man's arms before Violet was getting good at snuggling in and holding on.

"Tuck your face into my neck. Some of what is out front hasn't been cleared away yet and it's more than any decent woman should see. So please, close your eyes. I will have you past it in no time at all."

She did as he directed, although his declaration that whatever lay beyond was "more" than she could take rankled her some. His assumption that women were somehow less able to weather tragedy revealed how little he knew.

But she closed her eyes and nestled her face against his neck. Chin stubble grazed her cheek as she inhaled the now-familiar fragrances of the man.

The trip from outdoors to in was brief. Even though the wall of warmth that hit them when they entered the front hall was marvelous, she would have gladly traded it for a while longer in his arms.

"You can open your eyes now." He carried her into a parlor. When he set her onto her feet, she remembered she had been in dirt.

Violet looked down. The dark blue rug would probably conceal a lot but that didn't mean she should contribute to its destruction.

"I am filthy." She looked around the room and

noted an air of disuse. It was clean with simple furnishings, but there were no personal touches in evidence. No half-read books on a side table, embroidery lying on a footstool waiting for someone to come add a few stitches, or even a pair of slippers set discreetly beside the hearth. A spinning wheel occupied one corner without any sign of work in progress. The basket beside it held some blue wool but nothing more that she could see.

A fire in the hearth warmed the space. Had her feet not been dirt-covered she would have moved to stand closer. Instead, she remained where he'd placed her and wondered what to do next. Wrapping her arms across her chest, she gazed at her host.

He turned to leave. "I'm going to get your garments."

"Where are they? I can get them myself—you've already done too much for me."

He paused in the doorway. Turning back to meet her gaze, he shook his head. "It's best if you stay here. There are—well, there are things in the house that you shouldn't see. Let me get your garments, and then I'll take you home."

When he left, she wondered what lay beyond the door he closed behind him.

Had she been in a questionable home all along? Did he have something terrible to hide, something he was afraid she might tell others about?

Violet shook her head, annoyed with herself. Father had warned her about her overactive imagination more than once. It was time to heed his words.

At least hers wasn't as active as Daisy's. That her sister even wrote fiction and had it published—in secret, of course—proved almost intolerable to their parents. Violet was amused by her older sister's wild writing ways, but her parents definitely did not share the sentiment.

Her imagination would never rival Daisy's, although it was difficult to stop pondering what hid beyond the closed door.

Whatever her host concealed was none of her concern.

She needed to dress and leave. Her own home might be in peril from whatever deplorable men had already terrorized this part of Wylder. She had to go—and quickly.

He knocked on the door before opening it. She hadn't moved, so he walked over and handed her a bundle of clothing. "We need to get a wiggle on so the sheriff's men can come in and take care of business." He looked down at her feet, then met her gaze. "And don't worry none about a little bit of dirt. There's much worse on some of the floorboards in this place right now, so don't concern yourself with those pretty little toes of yours. Dress, and when you're ready, knock on the door. I'll come back in and get you, and then we'll get out of here."

He didn't wait for a reply.

She watched as he walked out. Despite Father's admonitions, she wondered what on earth was on the floorboards.

Those gunshots she'd heard weren't warning shots. Perhaps they had found a home—and spilled some blood.

Chapter 12

Thomas brought her coat, boots, scarf, hat, gloves, and bag so Violet layered the garments on as fast as she could manage. Her fingers were clumsy and her head felt filled with fog, but she got everything in place in minutes.

Her nightdress was destroyed but it did not matter. It had been intended to impress a man she had never loved on a night that had never happened, so why suffer any remorse over its ruin? She wadded it into a messy bundle and stuffed it into her book bag.

The red ribbon she remembered seeing wet and frozen was now clean, ironed, and rolled neatly in the bag.

Had he done all that? Washed her clothes, fixed and straightened her belongings?

It was far more likely Gertie had done the job. Her host did not seem prone to household duties…but she did not see a woman's touch in the place. Granted, she had only been privy to the sickroom and this one but there were no female footsteps or laughter since she had been a guest.

If a woman resided here, it seemed likely she would have brought meals or checked on Violet. The one who had done so was the man who, even now, paced outside the door. His bootsteps on the floorboards beat out an impatient cadence.

Violet took a last look around the empty room. Life was meant to be shared. It did not appear that the man of this house had anyone to share it with.

A sharp rap at the door cut short her musings. "Miss Bloom, are you ready? We need to leave."

What time was it? Hours in the cellar seemed endless and now minutes sped by. The darkness outside the window indicated it was still well before dawn.

Time made absolutely no sense right now. In truth, not much did.

She crossed to the door. "I am ready to go."

The door opened and she stood gazing up at the man she'd met a short time ago—but who was, for now, the only person in her life. And her life might once again depend on him.

He assessed every inch of her, from the hat on her head to the tips of her boot-clad toes. He gave a satisfied nod. "I will carry you outside. My horse is saddled and waiting."

"I am perfectly capable of walking. You don't need to carry me."

He shook his head, not meeting her gaze. "I'm sorry, but I can't let you do that. Not in your state."

Her brow furrowed. "My state?"

"Giant steps and slick surfaces…well, you're not in a good state of dress to tackle those situations. So, I'll carry you out—and I suggest you close your eyes again. Bury your face against my neck if that helps."

Violet held her bag close to her chest and allowed him to pick her up. He cradled her in his arms, and they stared into each other's eyes for a silent minute before she squeezed hers shut and leaned into the collar of his coat.

In less time than it took her to dress, they were outdoors. An Appaloosa waited at the hitching post. So did two other horses and their riders. In the darkness, Violet didn't get a decent look at the men.

"We good to go in now?" asked a deep voice.

"Lock the door when you're done. And don't forget the upstairs situation."

"Don't worry, we'll get everything. Won't clean up but we'll remove."

"That's enough."

As they dismounted, Thomas lifted her onto the back of his big horse, placing her sideways, so she gripped the pommel and held tightly while he mounted behind her.

Every southern woman could ride so this was not a new experience. However, she had never had a man pressed so intimately against her before.

It was strange and exhilarating all at once. She wanted to lean back against him, although she held herself straight while he turned the horse around. There had been too many indelicacies between them already. Her reputation was at stake, and she was conscious of the tongues that would wag if these two men took it into their heads to let on they'd seen her carried from a man's house in the dead of night.

His hands were on the reins and she sat in the circle of his arms. For an instant she almost forgot what had brought them to this moment.

Then she heard the two men coming back out of Thomas's house.

A loud thud, much like a heavy boot heel, came from the wooden front porch.

"Hey, watch his head, Jack."

"Hell, he ain't goin' to be needin' it where he's going."

Chapter 13

Violet drew a relieved breath when, at last, the horse turned onto her street.

She wanted to be home, away from the excitement of the past few days. Her life, with its dull schoolteacher routine, uneventful nights, and spending time with Ginny, called to her heart.

There were four houses on the little street, and she couldn't wait for the horse to get to hers. As they approached, she searched for signs that the rowdy ranch hands had come this way but thankfully didn't see any. Everything seemed as calm and quiet as usual.

She exhaled a breath she didn't know she'd been holding.

The house had been hers for a short time, but she was already attached to it. Had something gone wrong while she was away, her heart would have broken. She would be homeless, which was one of her worst fears.

Having a home gave a person substance. Mother had told her so, and she believed it to be true.

The horse went straight to the back of the house.

"He appears to know the way."

"We've been here before, remember?" Thomas dismounted and wrapped the reins around the hitching post near the back door.

By the time he turned to help her down, Violet had dismounted and was patting the horse's neck. "Thank you for giving me this midnight ride."

She went to the back door, turned, and looked at the man who had done right by her for days now. "Thank you for bringing me home. And thank you for all you've done for me." She paused, covering a yawn with the back of her left hand. "Pardon me. I didn't get much sleep so if you'll excuse me—"

He removed his hat and ran a hand through his thick, dark locks. "It's like this: I can't go back for a bit yet, maybe not for a couple of hours. The sheriff and his men are there, and they don't need any help from me. I'd greatly appreciate it if you would consider extending some hospitality to me."

What could she say?

The debt put her at his disposal, so she stepped across the threshold and held the door. "Of course. Welcome to my home."

"Thank you kindly." He stepped inside and she closed the door behind him.

It was a first, having a gentleman caller in the house. She had daydreamed about entertaining a kind man one day, but the notion had never included darkness or a caller who had already seen her in several indecent situations.

But one could not choose every detail of one's life, as she knew too well.

Violet sighed. Nowhere else felt as comfortable as one's own home.

She lit the candle that sat in its silver holder in the center of the kitchen table. Three candleholders had journeyed west with her. All were gifts from her sisters, and each meant the world to Violet. Every time she lit one, she imagined the light of her first home had made its way here.

She felt her sisters' love when she used the few belongings that came from them. How desperately she missed those three women. Even Lily, with her snooty ways.

Her house was humble, but it suited her purposes.

Simple construction made the dwelling cozy. On the first floor there were two rooms, neither could be considered large, formed by a single wall erected in the center of the house. It cut the space in half to form the main rooms. There were two smaller rooms, as well, and a staircase that hugged the northern wall.

Violet led the way into the front parlor, where she found two surprises. The first was the slow-burning fire in the fireplace.

She turned to Thomas. "Did you do this?"

"I did. I kept it banked down so you would have some hot coals to come home to."

Pointing to a huge stack of firewood beside the hearth, she asked, "And that?"

"I couldn't very well leave you to fetch wood after falling the way you did. Coyote said it would take a bit before you're in the pink again. I was being neighborly."

Neighborly. So that's what he called it?

Her throat tightened. She didn't deserve his care.

Thankfully, the second surprise took that moment to make herself known.

Two ears showed above the back of the chair closest to the fire.

"Ginny—my sweet girl." She lifted the cat, who stretched in greeting, and buried her face in its ginger-colored fur. "I missed you."

Violet sat down in the chair and held the cat on her lap. Ginny purred so loudly that their visitor chuckled. He squatted by the fire and pushed at the coals with the iron stick intended for that purpose. "It sounds like she missed you as much. I wondered about her name when I came to feed her. Ginny, eh?"

"Of course. She came all the way from Charleston with me by stagecoach. What else would a respectable southern beauty be called? She is like all South Carolinian women, graceful but with an iron will. At least, that's what Father says about us."

Thomas busied himself with the fire.

When he did not respond, she added, "Except that my father has never seen any of his daughters go flying through a snowstorm to land in a very unladylike and completely graceless lump in a snowbank."

He turned and sat on the stone hearth with his back to the fire. The flames were robust, generating ample heat into the room.

After placing his hat on the table beside him, he unbuttoned his coat. "You are too hard on yourself by far. Anyone who came on that icy patch would have slipped. Whatever were you doing out so early, anyhow? And on such a snowy morning, at that?"

She followed his lead and unbuttoned her coat. It wasn't an effortless endeavor, with the cat lounging on her lap, but she slipped her arms out of the garment, unwound her scarf, and dropped her hat onto the floor at her feet.

"I was headed to the schoolhouse. I thought I told you that—or did I dream that part?"

"No, you told me as much. But I still haven't figured out why you were going there so early. Surely your pupils can't arrive before sunrise."

"They don't. But I haven't much time to get the Christmas party decorations made, or the gifts done, or the preparations in the schoolroom attended to. There's so much to do—and I have been planning for this for two months already. Imagine if I left it for the last minute."

A log in the fire popped, as if to punctuate her words.

"Surely your pupils help you attend to such things, don't they?"

She stroked the kitty between the ears, where Ginny liked best. "They do, but frankly, we don't have a huge population in Wylder. Even with frontier families sending their children to school, I don't have a full classroom. There is more work to do than hands to do it all, sometimes."

He eyed her speculatively, scraping a palm across his chin. "Has it always been your life's ambition to teach in a schoolhouse on the frontier?"

She considered shielding the truth from the polite inquiry but was too tired to make the effort.

Most likely they would never have another conversation after this one. In the future, they would pass on the street, perhaps she would nod her head in recognition while he might tip his hat, and that would be the extent of their acquaintance.

She had no reason to believe that whatever she said now would matter one bit to this man, so she told the truth. "Not really, no. As a child, I watched my mother care for a home, children, and a husband, and wanted the same. A career, if you want to know the truth, didn't occur to me until I grew up."

He furrowed his brow. "Then why become a schoolteacher at all if you wanted to be a wife and mother?"

"I saw the war and its aftermath. So many men didn't return to their families. I watched women struggle. Most had no way to support themselves. I knew from a young age that I had to learn something that would keep me and my children fed if ever their father was killed. So, I became a teacher."

"Your whole life was changed by what you saw as a child." His words were soft and his shoulders dropped.

"The Union taught us southern women a lot of things, I'm afraid. I learned that I can never rely on a man to see me through. I will never, ever trust a Union soldier. Never."

He looked up at her. "But the war is over. Surely you can't hold a grudge this long."

"Oh, sir, I can. And, I do."

Chapter 14

When Violet woke, sunlight peeked through the front window beside her chair. Ginny nestled on her lap and the fire burned low in the hearth. Her coat had been spread over her lower legs and feet, which were propped on a footstool.

They were alone.

Scratching the cat between its ears, she said, "Well it looks like we're back to it being the two of us. We don't mind, do we? Men add too much confusion to life, anyway."

She glanced at the sky beyond the window. Cornflower blue, with slashes of pink across it. The Wyoming territory's skies were stunning, so vivid and soulful that she let her gaze rest on the sight for a long moment.

She put Ginny on the footstool and stood.

"Sorry, kitty of mine, but I'm running behind. If I hurry, I may get some of the decorations for the tree made. I may—that is, if I get a wiggle on and don't fall in the snow on the way to the schoolhouse."

Get a wiggle on.

Before last night, the only one who had ever said those words to her were Father, and that had been when she was a child.

She smiled and headed for her bedroom. It was comforting to hear a piece of home out here. Very comforting, indeed.

In less than twenty minutes she had bundled up and left for the schoolhouse. The walk was drastically different from the last trek she'd made between the two points. Now, the sun shone. Cold air kissed her cheeks, but the icy blasts and biting snow were gone.

The schoolhouse steps had already been cleared when she arrived. The straw broom used for that purpose stood beside the front door.

Violet pushed the door open and entered the familiar space.

Benches and desks formed rows on either side of a center aisle. Her heavy wooden desk, chair, and a recitation bench sat at the front of the room.

The pot-bellied stove took up space between the two side rows. She expected it to be cold, and the room freezing, but neither was true. She walked to the stove, pulled off one glove, and held her hand close to the warm cast iron.

Someone had started the fire.

Probably the same person who swept the steps off.

But who?

There wasn't time to puzzle over who showed such kindness. Having the chores done for her was a godsend. Now she could devote herself to the decorations.

The last few days had thrown her off schedule. Time to get back on it.

A closet in the corner of the room held her meager collection of school supplies. There was a coat hook in the closet, as well as room to store her personal belongings. She went there now, lifted the iron latch on the door, and opened it.

"Oh, my!" She dropped her bag, gloves, and hat on the floor.

A petite figure stared at her from the closet's interior. Black hair framed an oval face. Almond-shaped eyes met her gaze.

Although she herself had recently spent time hidden in a closet of sorts, she did not expect to see someone in one of her own.

What does one say to a closeted person?

"Well, hello. Ah, good morning."

The barest of smiles and a chin nod.

"Well, did you clear the schoolhouse steps and kindle the fire?"

Another chin nod.

"Would you like to come out? You must be very cramped in there."

Dark eyes gazed at the floor, then peeked into the empty classroom. Violet felt apprehension as tangibly as if it had been written in ink on the other's forehead. Words were not necessary.

She rushed to reassure. "There is no one here. It is a while before any pupils will arrive. Please, come out of there."

Violet stood back, folded her hands at her waist, and did her best to look as unformidable as possible.

Chinese laborers were a common sight in Wylder. Many worked on the railways. Some held positions in various businesses, usually sweeping floors, unloading wagons, or doing other laborious tasks. They helped keep the economy, and the town itself, running.

Seeing Chinese workers in town did not surprise her. Finding one in her teaching closet did.

She had heard that there were even a few Chinese

women working at the Wylder Social Club, but she did not know if that was fact or fiction. It was merely gossip, something she could not avoid overhearing but did not herself spread. Whether or not those women worked at the Social Club was none of her concern.

The unexpected visitor emerged. They eyed one another warily.

She didn't know what this intruder's intentions were, or if they were nefarious. Violet had her derringer in her skirt. With what she hoped was a harmless movement, she placed her right hand in the pocket. It would be better if she didn't need to use the weapon, but it wouldn't do to erroneously believe this person meant her no harm.

Now that she was confident she could handle whatever arose, she decided introductions were in order. This wasn't Charleston but social niceties should be kept if possible. Mother had drummed that into her daughters' heads and Violet hadn't forgotten it.

"I'm Miss Bloom, the schoolteacher here." A nod was the reply she received so she pushed on. "And you are?"

The visitor looked toward the door and for an instant Violet thought they might make a run for it.

"Sun Lin."

It was difficult to know for certain whether the person standing in her schoolroom was male or female. The drab, loose-fitting black shirt, trousers, and jacket were standard on the immigrant work force. A knitted cap was pulled down low over the forehead, but there was something in the eyes that made her doubt the person was a man. There was a raw beauty lurking in the gaze.

Violet took a chance. "Miss Lin?"

Dark eyes rounded. They stared at each other long enough for the snow on Violet's boots to melt off and create a puddle on the floorboards.

A very small nod of acknowledgement. "No one know. They no know I not a man."

Words failed Violet. This woman masqueraded as a man, obviously. But why? And how?

"Do you work somewhere? Do they think you are a man, is that it?"

"Yes."

"Is someone looking for you? Did you leave your job—and now they are looking for you?"

The slender woman's shoulders sagged. "No one to look. Brother dead. I leave when brother die. No one left."

Her heart shattered for Sun Lin. She had known loneliness, but she also had a family, which it appeared this woman might not have.

"Do you have family here? Or in China?"

A slow tear rolled down her cheek. "No family. No one left. Only me."

Chapter 15

Violet would have preferred Miss Lin not return to the closet but when she suggested as much, the diminutive woman dropped to her knees and begged to be allowed back into the hiding spot. Since she didn't know what else to do, Violet agreed—but only after feeding the woman the cheese and bread she had brought for her own lunch and making a soft nest with the extra coat and sweater she kept in the closet.

When the earliest buckboard rattled into the schoolyard, she reluctantly shut the door to the closet. Violet said a quick appeal that the day would be gentle to the hidden soul. And that by day's end, she would have devised a plan to help the woman.

Thirty-two students arrived at the schoolhouse in a flurry, as was the norm. Some walked from homes in town while others rode in wagons over snowy lanes. They all showed up before she rang the bell and were excited to see each other as well as their teacher.

Brian Sweetwater looked older than his twelve years, all rough, tumble, and swagger but the child had the heart of an angel. It garnered lots of teasing from his peers, but his biceps were threat enough to keep the others from getting too far out of hand. Violet doubted Brian would ever hit another pupil, but she applauded his ingenuity. Putting a bit of fear into those who taunted him was wise. It kept him safe—and he never had to resort to using those muscles.

He rode a wagon with his sister and younger brother, along with the children of the ranch hands who worked his father's land. He helped his younger brother get situated at his desk near the front of the room before walking shyly up the center aisle to her desk.

Brian stood on the other side and waited for her to address him.

"Good morning, Brian."

"'Morning, Miss Bloom." He brought a hand from behind his back and placed a fabric-wrapped item on her blotter. "My mama sent this. Said she's sorry to hear you're feeling poorly. She hopes you're doin' better. She said this'll help get your blood back to rights."

"Why, thank you." Violet unwrapped the fabric to find one beautiful orange. "What a considerate gift! Please be sure to tell your mother that I'm very grateful. And she's right, I do believe this will help get my blood back in order."

"Yes'm. I'll tell her." He shot her a shy smile, turned, and walked to his place. He was a row behind his brother, being older. Violet watched him give the youngest Sweetwater a fast wave as he passed.

Someday she hoped to have children of her own. For now, watching others' offspring would have to do.

At nine o'clock sharp, she stood and began the school day.

As she handed out the McGuffey Readers, she wondered how the woman hiding in the coat closet was faring.

Violet had no idea how Miss Lin had pretended to be a man or how her brother died, but she knew she had to find a way to help her. From her fear of discovery, it was clear that the woman believed someone wanted to find her. Her shaking hands and plea for concealment showed that she thought discovery would lead to punishment—or worse.

She might only be the spinster schoolteacher, but Violet would be damned if she allowed anyone to hurt an innocent woman. She had to find a way to save the unfortunate soul—even if that meant she'd have to hide her for a while longer.

Chapter 16

Winter months typically saw more boys than girls in the schoolhouse.

Girls populated the schoolroom in greater numbers during the sweet, warm months. They were needed for chores, but unlike their brothers they could be spared a day or two a week for some formal schooling.

In December, though, some families allowed their daughters to venture forth in order that they not miss out on the season's festivities. There weren't a lot of reasons for widespread celebrating in the territory, but Christmas and the upcoming new year were events that made memories and gave them something to talk about for the other eleven months.

Come January, daily attendance would drop again but for these pre-holiday weeks Violet anticipated extra pupils in her schoolroom. She wished the desks could stay filled all year but understood why that was impractical.

She cherished this time and vowed to make it as exciting for all her young learners as she could. During these weeks she typically kept them in the schoolroom as late in the afternoon as possible.

But today, when she wanted everyone to depart in a timely manner so she might release the woman in her closet, the opposite happened.

First, the youngest Leonard boy misplaced his

pencil. As they each had one pencil it caused a search of the schoolroom floor. The eldest Leonard boy, Charlie, offered to sweep to locate the missing item.

When he went to open the closet, Violet ran across the room to stop him. His hand was on the latch as she threw her back against the door. "No! Don't open that!"

Charlie's eyes grew huge. The child was sandy-haired, a slender young boy and when he pulled his hand away, he took a step back.

She had frightened him. But she couldn't allow anyone to discover Sun Lin.

"I'm sorry, ma'am. I thought if we swept up, we might find Ed's pencil."

"Ah, yes, that is a fine idea. However, on days like today I sweep the floor myself."

His brow creased. "Days like today, ma'am? What kind of day is that?"

The child hardly ever had a correct answer prepared when she called on him. And when he stood at the front of the class to recite, he stammered his way through even the simplest passages from the readers.

Yet here he stood, asking questions and thinking things out like a politician.

"Thursday. I like to sweep on Thursdays, Charlie."

"Ma'am?"

She heard the barest sound from within the closet and hoped Charlie didn't hear it, as well.

Violet raised her voice a notch to drown out any more closet sounds. "Yes, Charlie? What is it?"

He took another step back when she spoke. Today was a day of surprises for her young charge. First, she ran across the room, and now she raised her voice. They were two things she did not generally do.

But this was not an ordinary day.

And she wished the three lagging pupils would find the pencil and leave already.

"Do you always like to sweep on Thursdays? It seems to me that last Thursday—"

Delighted cries came from the area near the front door.

"Found it!" The middle boy, Davey, held the pencil in the air.

Ed reached for it, but his brother wasn't done waving the find, which resulted in a minor scuffle.

Violet put a hand on Charlie's shoulder and walked him toward his siblings.

"Boys, stop that this instant. Davey, give the pencil to Ed and go on home now. Your mother's bound to wonder what's keeping you." She crossed her arms and tried to look stern.

She must have succeeded because the pencil made its way to its owner and the brothers exited the building. She waited until she heard their laughter subside before she hurried to the closet and put her hand on the door latch.

"Well, hello, Miss Bloom. I hope you don't mind my stopping in."

Damn.

She put her forehead against the door for an instant before straightening and turning to the front of the schoolroom.

Thomas Harvey, holding his hat in one hand and a paper-wrapped bundle in the other, grinned.

Suddenly the room felt smaller than it had.

And she was perspiring. In December? It was unheard of.

Except now, when she stood as shocked and still as a statue and hoped he could not see the sheen breaking out on her temples.

Chapter 17

"Mister Harvey."

He tipped his head. "Miss Bloom."

Lingering with him wasn't an option today. She had a very pressing concern to attend to. He had to leave.

Her chest felt as if it contained a salmon that had landed on a riverbank. There were lots of flipping and not-so-subtle flopping sensations taking place beneath her skin.

It was almost nauseating, this strange feeling.

But it was a favorable kind of nauseous if that were possible.

Which, as the sensations in her body clearly showed, it was. Very possible.

Damn it all. He still had to go.

"Is there something I can do for you?" She hoped the expression on her face did not show the flip-flopping inside her as she clasped her hands at her waist and made her way over to him.

When she got close, the tobacco scent she remembered so fondly wafted over her. It was so masculine and, quite frankly, nearly intoxicating. She wanted to lean in and breathe the man into her lungs, hold him there, and savor the richness of him.

Something must be wrong with her. Had she knocked her head when she fell? Because she was surely addlepated. Her response to the man made no sense at all.

And it increased the activity of the salmon jumping inside her.

Yes, she must have hit her head.

"It's good to see you looking so well. I trust you have recovered sufficiently." He glanced around the big room. "Well enough, it appears, to resume your duties. I imagine your pupils were pleased to see you."

She looked about and tried to imagine what sort of impression the schoolroom might give someone who had never been inside the schoolhouse.

Not as neat as it had been when she walked in this morning, but still presentable. Desks were cleared, the pile of boots beside the stove was gone, and the children had placed all the readers back on the bookshelves in neat rows.

The remains of the day's lessons still covered her desk, with her grade book open beside two blue readers.

The orange peels from the gift she'd received this morning had gone on top of the stove. Now they were shriveled and blackened but had given off a summery, citrusy scent earlier.

She had yet to wipe the chalkboard clean of the verse of the day as well as the small homework assignment she had given.

"I am fine, thank you for asking. And yes, the pupils were as pleased to see me as I was to see them, I believe." She allowed her gaze to wander over his shoulders. They looked massive in the heavy denim coat he wore. The memory of his arms holding her close, of the way he lifted her so gently, and the recollection of how her face felt tucked against his neck made her body heat. She swallowed, and then cleared her throat, trying to move her mind from how it felt to be near the man to how to get him out of her schoolroom. "Ah, Mister Harvey…"

He grinned and for an instant she worried he could read her mind.

"Miss Bloom." His lips quirked up at the edges into a full smile. "I think we have already greeted each other formally. Now, it seems, we are riding in circles. I am not complaining, mind you, merely making an observation." His teasing tone warmed her heart and if she hadn't been intent on releasing Sun Lin, she would have loved to tease him right back.

But now was not the time.

"Yes, well, that is true. We are circling about." She looked pointedly over her shoulder toward her desk and waved a hand to the work waiting her attention. "As you can see, I have much to do before I can close up. Is there something I can help you with?"

He held the package out. When she grasped it, she knew what the wrapping enclosed. One did not become a schoolteacher without knowing the feel of a book.

"It is the volume of poetry you were reading when you stayed with me. I don't believe you had the chance to finish. As I know it is an exceptionally meaningful volume, I hoped you might wish to read on."

Tears pricked the backs of her eyes. It had been a long time since anyone had treated her so well.

"That is kind of you. I am grateful and will finish it quickly." A few days of reading beside the fire sounded like an ideal way to pass a winter weekend. "I shall have it back to you on Monday."

He shook his head. "No need to return the book. It

is a gift, one I hope will bring you joy."

A gift? Oh, but she couldn't accept anything from a man she barely knew.

"Why, Mister Harvey, it's not proper for me to keep your book. It is a delightful volume and is, undoubtedly, worth a good deal. I cannot possibly accept it. No, I must insist on returning it—either now or on Monday."

A muscle worked in his jaw as he stared at her. He opened his mouth once but closed it again. He glanced away, toward the window and whatever he imagined lay beyond the thick pane of glass.

Finally, he looked back at her. Their gazes locked. It surprised her to see his dark brown eyes had a sheen to them, almost as if he were holding back tears.

He spoke with tenderness. "I don't believe you can appreciate how necessary it is that you take my gift. You need not believe you are in any way indebted to me for having accepted the volume." He looked over her shoulder before returning his gaze to hers. "And, as I realize now that it would seem improper for an unmarried lady to receive favors from just any man about town, I will not divulge that I gave that to you. But please, keep the book. It is important to me that you do. Very important."

Did she imagine it, or did his voice hitch at the final two words?

The day's light departed as they spoke. Standing in the shadows, the man looked wholly tortured.

She could not hurt him or add to whatever sorrow plagued him.

"I accept the book, then. Gratefully."

He nodded and turned toward the door to leave.

While she needed him gone, she couldn't keep herself from asking a question.

"Please, can you tell me why it is so important that I take the book?"

The man had his back to her and he did not turn, but his shoulders fell.

"It belonged to someone special. She loved it and…" He paused and took a breath so deep it lifted his shoulders. "She read it many times. No one has read it since she left, and it seems that something so profound should be enjoyed. Beauty is not meant to be kept on a shelf."

Chapter 18

Violet locked the door the instant Mister Harvey departed. She dropped the heavy wooden bar down into the metal brackets on the inside of the frame, ensuring that no one could enter without battering it down.

She ran to the closet and yanked the door open.

Sun Lin stood just inside. When released, she ran for the back door without saying a word.

Oh, good Lord. It hit Violet that she should have thought to put a bucket in the closet. The poor woman must be in agony!

She did not wish to appear indelicate, so she went about clearing off her desk. She put the attendance roster in the top drawer. The readers she bookmarked for tomorrow's lessons before piling them on top of each other and putting them to one side. She sharpened her pencils and placed them in the cup beside her blotter.

With the desk organized, she washed the blackboard. While she waited for it to dry, she turned to the stove. She shoveled some of the day's ashes into the ash bucket before adding a few large pieces of wood to the belly stove and banking it down. There would be embers in the morning, and it would be fairly simple to breathe life into another fire tomorrow.

One day builds upon the next.

She grew anxious for Sun Lin's return. It felt like

forever since she'd left.

Maybe she should go check on her. Perhaps she had fallen in the snow…

But when she turned back from tending the stove, the other woman stood near the front of the room. She wore no coat and looked cold, so Violet motioned her over.

She stepped back, giving the newcomer the spot directly in front of the woodstove where the heat was most intense. She received a small smile and a nod for her kindness.

Sun Lin rubbed her hands together. She held them out to the stove, warming herself, and Violet saw how raw and chapped the woman's fingers were. She had not been living an easy life.

Mother always said that proper introductions showed the substance of a woman, so she began there.

"Our introductions were rushed earlier. Honestly, I don't recall whether I introduced myself. I'm Violet Bloom, the schoolteacher. And you are Miss Sun Lin—did I say that properly, Miss Lin?"

"Oh…yes. It is good how you speak. Thank you."

Communicating posed a challenge, but so far, they understood each other well enough.

"Is it 'Miss Lin' or 'Miss Sun'—I don't mean to be impolite, but I'm not really sure which is correct, and I would hate to be disrespectful and call you by the wrong name."

This lengthy statement brought a confused expression to the woman's face. Her eyes were the deepest shade of brown and her skin the most beautiful golden color, and Violet loved how delicately her eyebrows arched above soulful eyes.

Keep it simple.

"I am sorry. That was a lot."

If her parents could see her apologizing to a woman of another race, they surely would go apoplectic. They had owned slaves and believed they were not wrong for having done so. Neither Violet nor any of her sisters had been able to dissuade them, not even after they produced literature smuggled in from the north that gave valid reasons for why slavery should not exist.

Her parents came from generations of slave owners. They would not approve of one of their daughters apologizing to a Chinese person.

Her parents would not approve of her addressing Sun Lin at all.

But they were not here. She was of an age to know her own mind. And while she could not change her parents, she did not have to follow their rules or share their beliefs.

Violet put a hand on Sun Lin's shoulder. Hoping compassion might help bridge a language barrier, she gave a gentle squeeze. The bony shoulder made her wonder whether there had been enough food wherever the woman and her brother had been working. By the feel of the form beneath her hand, she doubted it.

She took her hand away and tried a different approach.

"I am Violet Bloom."

A nod. "Schoolteacher."

"Yes, that's right. I am the schoolteacher. The children call me Miss Bloom."

Sun Lin smiled for the first time since they had met. She nodded. "Mi Bloom."

Close enough.

Violet smiled and said, "Yes, that's right. And you are Sun Lin. Miss Lin, is that correct?"

The other tilted her head. Clearly, she attempted to translate to understand the question, so Violet waited.

Sun Lin shook her head. "No. No Mi Lin."

"Missus Lin? Are you married, then?"

At that, the woman put her hand in front of her mouth and giggled. She waved her free hand in the air between them and shook her head.

"No, no—no married."

Violet was thoroughly confused, although it pleased her to see Sun Lin find humor in the situation.

"So not married? Miss Lin is not married."

Sun Lin wiped laughter's tear from one cheek. "No Mi Lin." She placed a hand on the center of her chest. "Mi Sun."

Miss Sun, not Miss Lin. That must mean the names were somehow switched, in an arrangement unfamiliar to Violet.

She placed a hand over her own heart. "Violet."

Sun Lin mimicked her hand placement. "Lin."

They smiled at each other.

"Your name is Lin, then? Your first name?"

"Please, call me Lin."

Violet bobbed her head. "Then you must call me Violet." The effort of communicating nearly wore her out but she went on. "Lin, do you have a place to stay? Somewhere to sleep?"

A tentative head shake accompanied a pleading expression as she pointed toward the closet behind them.

She wanted to continue sheltering in the

schoolroom closet.

"No, that won't do at all." Violet put her hand back on her new friend's shoulder and said, "You will come home with me. There is plenty of room for you—and besides, you don't take up much space at all, do you? Lin, when did you last eat a decent meal? No, don't answer that—it doesn't matter. Let's get home before it gets dark, and we will have time to chat more later."

Chapter 19

In no time it became clear to Violet that she and Lin were going to get along. They did not speak on the short walk between the schoolhouse and Violet's home, mostly due to the brisk wind that nipped their cheeks and stole their breath. Darkness had descended by the time they made the proper street, and all women knew better than to linger outdoors after sundown in Wylder.

Females were not safe in the wild west on their own in the dark. Women accepted the fact, so Violet moved swiftly over the last stretch of icy ground, Lin hurrying to keep up.

Once inside, Violet relaxed. As she went to stoke the fire, Lin hung their coats and "woolens"—gloves, scarves, and hats—on the wooden rack beside the hearth. Any dampness would send some vapor into the air, as well as a faint wooly scent, as they dried.

"We need something warm for dinner. You must be very hungry, aren't you, Lin?" Violet's belly felt cavernous. An orange wasn't nearly enough to keep her, but since she had given her lunch to the other woman, it had been the day's sustenance.

She had some soup in a pot on the wood stove, so she got the fire going and began to set the table.

"Please, Lin, sit down. Over here, close to the stove where you will be warm."

Violet chose her words carefully. She didn't want

to overwhelm her guest again, and perhaps frighten her. No, her goal was to become friends and hopefully help the woman.

Lord knew, she needed someone to take her under a protective wing.

Violet could imagine how difficult it might be to find oneself fully alone in the world. Granted, she lived in the territory on her own, but she did have family back east. And she thought coming out west would be the turning point in her life, with husband and children in short order. It hadn't happened, but the promise of starting her own family had been enough to keep her traveling to Wylder, despite the shady circumstances surrounding her westward move.

Lin complied when invited to take a seat but, in a heartbeat, she rose to her feet again. She stood and adjusted the table settings, lining up bowls and spoons at precise angles.

Violet took the lid off the pot of simmering soup. Fragrant steam escaped into the air. As if on cue, her belly rumbled and they both giggled.

"Not very ladylike of me, I'm afraid. I apologize. It seems I am hungrier than I knew."

"Yes, hungry." Lin rubbed a hand over her midsection with a nod. "Hungry."

While Violet ladled generous helpings of piping hot vegetable soup into two ceramic bowls, she wondered how to broach any of the topics swirling through her mind. Helping someone without knowing their exact needs could prove tricky.

Lin required a place to stay. This house provided more than enough room for two unmarried women to occupy comfortably so that problem solved itself.

A good meal might loosen Lin's tongue. Then Violet would know if there were other ways she could support her new friend.

Two bowls of soup, some sourdough bread, and a small chunk of cheese made a hearty repast. She waited until they had taken several mouthfuls of soup before she cut the bread and offered a slice to her guest.

Lin looked ready to decline so Violet said, "Please, help yourself. I baked the bread a few days ago and if we don't eat it soon, it will get stale." The bread had been baked this morning before she went to the schoolhouse, but the tiny fib was harmless. It worked to convince Lin to take a slice of bread and a piece of cheese.

When their bowls were nearly empty, Violet considered her questions. She had a few but felt it best to ask the most essential ones first. Everything else could wait.

"I am sorry to learn about the loss of your brother. You must have been awfully close." She kept her tone gentle, mindful of the nature of the topic.

Lin stopped eating. She put her spoon in the bowl and stared down at her hands. When she spoke, Violet leaned forward to hear her words.

"Thank you. Yes. Very close."

"Ah, your brother. Did he have an illness?"

A perplexed expression crossed her companion's face so she rephrased the query.

"Your brother. Was he sick? Unwell?"

Violet put a hand to her forehead as if she were suffering from a fever. Then she coughed into her palm and sniffed to show illness.

It worked. The other woman shook her head.

"No. No sick—no ill. No…un…un…" She held her hand out, palm raised.

"Unwell," she supplied. "It is another word for sick or ill, unwell. There are really too many words in the language, if you ask me. One would suffice." She saw the confused expression on Lin's face so she stopped explaining. "Sick." Again, she pantomimed illness.

Lin nodded. "Sick."

"But your brother was not sick?"

"No." Another quick shake of the head. Now that Lin had removed her hat, her glossy black hair, pulled back into a sleek braid, shone in the candlelight. She shook her head so vigorously that the braid slid across her shoulder. "Not sick."

Violet took a deep breath and forged on. "How did your brother die, then? What happened to him, Lin? Can you tell me?"

Lin folded her hands in her lap again but this time she did not stare down at them. Instead, they locked gazes and studied each other for several heartbeats. Violet did her utmost to show that she meant no harm. She wanted the Chinese woman to see that her South Carolinian heart wasn't touched by an ounce of intolerance, so she concentrated on showing love and compassion through her gaze.

"Yes. I tell." She took a deep breath. Then, she sighed it out and closed her eyes tightly. They glistened when she opened them. Lin raised one hand, curled three fingers into her palm, held her pointer finger out and her thumb upright. She placed the pantomime of a gun in the air.

Lin turned the gun on herself, placed the tip of her finger in the center of her body above her heart, and pushed the thumb down. "Boom."

Chapter 20

Every woman had a limit to the amount of heartache she could inflict or witness. Violet saw how deeply Lin felt the loss of her brother and remembered how it felt to have Father return with the bodies of her brother and their close friends. Her heart ached for the woman, and she couldn't allow the conversation to continue much longer.

"I'm sorry, Lin. Truly, sorry. I lost a brother too. I understand."

Lin raised the hand again and pulled the imaginary trigger finger. "This way?"

She closed her eyes and nodded. "Yes, my brother was shot to death, too."

"I am sorry, Mi Bloom."

The lyrical pronunciation of her name brought a small smile. "Violet, remember? We are friends and you need not call me anything more than that."

"Violet."

"Very good, then. Why don't we clear the dishes and retire to the parlor? We can talk some more or we can rest. Although, I do have some Christmas decorations I need to attend to. Honestly, those children today were scatterbrained, the whole lot of them. Losing pencils, reading poorly from their readers, spelling like wild animals—I don't know what's come over any of them, really I don't."

She babbled as she carried dishes to the dish pan. She missed the companionship of her three sisters. All her life she took their presence, long talks, shared laughter, and friendship for granted. Now she yearned for all of it.

Lin didn't speak much, but she did not seem to mind listening. Violet thought that the more the other woman heard English, the greater her chances of learning to speak fluently became.

The house had a water pump in the kitchen, a true luxury. She had envisioned going outdoors to some sort of holding tank for the household water. After all, this was the frontier. But the home had a few nice surprise conveniences, including the indoor pump.

Violet splashed water into a pot which she set on the stove to heat. A bit of soup remained so she left it in place. If she added a cup or two of water and a potato, there would be enough to feed them tomorrow.

She had no intention of allowing Lin to leave on her own, with no family at all, and no prospects of staying safe and healthy. The woman needed people to call her own and Violet decided to step up and become Lin's family.

Maybe they would become as close as sisters. She daydreamed so long the water began to boil so she took it from the stove and dumped half into the wash basin before setting the hot pot back. Another splash from the pump to the wash water and she went to work. There were soup dishes and spoons, so it went quickly.

Their tea was steeping in the pot she brought all the way from Charleston. Now she reached for the biscuit tin and shook it. Not many, but enough for them to enjoy one each. The occasion should be festive.

While Violet washed, dried, and put away the dishes, Lin swept the floor.

It took no time at all for the room to be immaculate. Violet lifted the tea tray and nodded to the candle. "Do you mind blowing that out, please?" She pursed her lips and blew, to show what she meant. Lin blew the candle out and followed Violet into the front room.

They sat, each in a chair by the fire.

Violet looked at the hearth, to the place where a short time ago Thomas Harvey had perched. She recalled the way his form obscured her view of the far side of the hearth, the way his shoulders were so broad that they seemed to fill a doorway, and how wonderful it had been to have a man around.

She'd felt safe with him, even when he locked her in a cupboard or dug her out of a hole in the ground. It was strange, but she hadn't ever been afraid. Not really.

Well, not much.

Forget it. What's done is done and the past cannot be relived.

They drank their tea and ate their biscuits in silence.

After they'd emptied the teapot, Violet brought over a basket of pinecones, ribbons, and fabric scraps. Lin looked questioningly at the assortment so she took a pinecone, wrapped some fabric around its base, and tied a ribbon onto it so it could be hung.

"Christmas decorations, for the big party at the schoolhouse. The whole town will be there—all of Wylder, as well as the families from the closest ranches and homesteads. I need to get these decorations done. I want there to be enough so that everyone who attends will take one home with them—a little gift to the folks who have been so nice."

She put the decoration into an empty basket. Violet picked up another pinecone and some fabric.

Lin reached for supplies. Her hand stopped over the basket and she asked, "Yes?"

"Oh, yes, please. I would love your help."

Lin gathered a pinecone and some supplies onto her lap. She watched the process a second time, and then began working on hers. When she was done, she held it up and Violet clapped with delight.

"That is gorgeous. Lin, you have an artistic eye—that is so much prettier than the ones I have been making. Now I'm going to watch and take a lesson from you."

Violet handed more materials to the other woman and took some for herself. They traded ideas and methods of wrapping ribbon between the pinecone petals, and the evening passed in wonderful, sister-like contentment.

For a little while, both forgot their journeys had been difficult, that aside from each other they were alone in a dangerous, rugged town, or that come tomorrow neither knew what new, and potentially difficult, situation waited. The pleasure they found in sitting side by side, chatting about colored ribbons and scraps of patterned fabric while they created homespun masterpieces was a gift.

Violet pushed all the lingering questions about Lin from her mind. She did not allow any trepidation over the woman's situation or how she was going to resolve it infringe on their happiness.

She also did not let herself think about Thomas

Harvey too awful much.

No, that was a lie.

Violet strived to keep from contemplating her association with the man, but her attempts were futile.

Even while she and Lin chatted in the stilted manner that two people who don't truly understand each other fall into, Violet heard the man's voice in her head, felt his body against hers, and could still imagine the scent of him.

It was the first time a man infiltrated her private thoughts this way.

She rather liked it—although it was, in a word, startling.

Chapter 21

On Friday school started an hour later than on other days of the week.

Some homesteaders gathered in a round-robin fashion on Thursday evenings to help each other with bigger projects that required a tad more muscle or some extra hands. Homesteading was tough and they assisted when they could.

Sometimes projects required late nights.

Early rising on the frontier was essential but when last evening's chores waited on Friday morning because aiding another was also essential, getting to school dropped down the priority list.

It wasn't standard procedure but giving leeway where needed seemed a small price to pay to keep attendance up. Had Violet not allowed for the later start, she wouldn't have the homesteaders' children in her schoolroom on Fridays.

She liked the extra hour to herself. Usually she stayed home and lingered over her morning household duties but today there was no need.

Lin agreed to live at the house. It had taken a bit to convince her but finally Violet succeeded. Lin would stay—but she insisted on doing her share to help with the household chores.

By the time she returned this afternoon Violet expected her cozy home would be cleaner than it had ever been. When she left, Lin polished the wooden banister with such absorption she barely noticed Violet opening the front door.

With Christmas one day closer and her preparation list still longer than her arm, she went straight to the mercantile. Supplies were limited, especially during the winter months, so she hoped to find what she still needed.

The railroad brought in much of the town's goods, but even that remained less reliable in the snowy season. During a recent blizzard, a derailment outside Wylder scattered cargo that quickly became snow-covered. It would be spring before two railroad cars and their loads were recovered.

The clear sky didn't match the soft blue skies seen in summer, but it wasn't a foreboding, gray one, either. A compromise between the two filled Violet with gratitude. The week had begun with a stormy sky and her flying into a snowbank. Much better to end it on a higher note.

Wylder Mercantile, on Wylder Street, stood directly across from the hotel. A hulking wooden two-story structure, it made its nearest neighbor, Lowery's Dress Shop, look slight by comparison.

The Wylder family, who built and owned the huge mercantile, meant it to be a focal point in town, and they'd succeeded. A slatted walkway ran the front length of the building. Cedar hitching posts accommodated horses and mules.

Last summer a circus traveled through town. For a whole day, two camels were hitched in front of the mercantile to advertise the circus's presence. Almost every citizen in town gathered and gawked, but no one had the heart to tell the owner that they were all aware the big tents were visiting. A few brave souls stepped up to pet the exotic creatures.

Now there were no camels tied to the posts. A lone pack mule with a fur tossed over its neck to keep the chill off its sturdy little body stood waiting patiently for its owner.

Violet stamped her feet outside to get the worst of the snow and grime off her boots. Then she pushed on the wide door and stepped inside.

She loved this business because it reminded her of home. Not fancy like so many of the southern shops were, but with a comfortable atmosphere to it, like Babbitt's Mercantile on Charleston Street. Father ordered supplies for his business there, and she had accompanied him into Babbitt's from an early age. Back then, he bought her a peppermint stick for the walk home. Those moments with him were treasures, and any reminders of gentle times back in South Carolina warmed her heart.

She moved to the dry goods section to see what bits of ribbon and fripperies she might find to fancy up her decorations. Hopefully, the selection wouldn't be too picked over.

If she were in Charleston with her sisters, she would be busy sewing gifts, stringing garlands, and concocting all manner of festive fun for family and friends. This season away from home felt so different from everything she knew that it hardly felt like Christmastime at all. If it weren't for the town gathering, she wouldn't have one holiday item on her to-do list.

Luck smiled on her. Ribbons remained on the

shelf. Some bright yellow caught her attention, as did a dark green. She pushed aside the upper layer to dig deeper into the selection and found some red and mint green. They would do just fine to finish wrapping pinecones.

A bushel basket filled with folded remnants, the ends of bolts of fabrics too short to use as full yard goods, provided more decorating promise. Violet picked pink and lavender floral fabrics as well as some sturdy blue denim. The florals would make pretty dresses for dolls for the girls and the denim suited the pencil cases she intended for her male pupils. She added buttons for closures on the pencil cases and went toward the counter to settle up.

Violet paused when she passed the clothing. She had given Lin one of her everyday dresses, a sweater, and the other necessary items to see her comfortably attired. The poor woman owned one set of clothing, and they were men's garments.

She picked out undergarments and a nightdress. Thinking of the deep brown eyes of her newest friend, she chose a wrapper decorated with swirls of brown and green embroidery along its edges. Satisfied that they would make Lin feel welcome, she carried them to the counter with her other items.

While she shopped, the store gained some customers. She passed a young mother with a screaming toddler in tow and managed to smile and nod without having to stop to chat. Sometimes an unruly child did make escaping meaningless conversations uncomplicated.

Carlotta Dade, a farmer's widow rumored to be quick on the draw, stood near the coffee when Violet walked by. Vernon Dade was one of her pupils, so she stopped to speak with the widow.

"Missus Dade, it's nice to see you. You're looking well."

The woman appeared hale and hearty. Her son had been robust recently, as well. Rumors that the widow had begun keeping company with a cowboy who treated her and the young boy real well circulated about town. Violet hoped they were true.

"Thank you, Miss Bloom. And yourself, you look fine, too. I have been meanin' to thank you for teaching my Vern so good. He's really getting quick with his sums, isn't he?"

While the woman's grammar lacked finesse, her enthusiasm and appreciation were authentic.

She had reason to be proud of her son. When Violet met Vern, the twelve-year-old could barely write his own name. His father had been killed in a farming accident, which the boy had witnessed. The child suffered the loss in a prolonged state of devastation. But she had worked with him, had been sympathetic and loving, and bit by bit he came back to his senses.

Now he could read and write at the proper level. His arithmetic still lagged, but time would take care of that.

Violet thought it must be difficult to raise a boy, care for a farm, and grieve a husband. The woman deserved every bit of understanding society could throw her way.

"Vern is doing very well in all of his subjects. You should be pleased. He has shown such improvement— and I'm certain he will continue to do well into the spring term."

"Oh, I sure hope you're right. His pa would be happy if he could see him now. I know he would. He'd be real proud."

Violet smiled, nodded in agreement, and wished Missus Dade a good day before she went to the front counter.

Time grew short so she did not stop to chat with anyone else. In fact, she even showed Finn Wylder, the owner of the mercantile, her brisk side. She didn't mean to be rude, but she couldn't dilly-dally. With her hour nearly up, she had to go ready the school for her pupils.

Finn towered over her slight frame, a pleasant man with light brown hair and gentle brown eyes.

"Thank you, Mister Wylder." Violet took her change and tucked it into her reticule. "Good day."

"Good day, Miss Bloom."

"Well, isn't it a coincidence we meet on such a beautiful morning?" The familiar tobacco scent wafting her way could have been from the display beside the counter, but she knew better.

She looked up into the eyes that had invaded her dreams these past few nights.

"Mister Harvey."

"Miss Bloom." He removed his hat and tipped his head. "Yes, I do say, this is a fine coincidence."

"Coincidence? Why, whatever do you mean?"

"Oh, just that it is a lovely day—and you are one of Wylder's loveliest ladies."

She colored. Fortunately, the only one in earshot was the man behind the counter.

Then she remembered Carlotta Dade. Had the woman heard him? No way of knowing so Violet kept her chin high and wished she could grab her goods and run.

He glanced down at the items she had purchased and grinned. She followed his gaze and saw the white underclothes on top of the pile that the merchant began to bundle in plain paper.

Her cheeks heated.

The things she chose for Lin were practical, unadorned, and cotton. They were what she thought the woman would fancy, although their communication skills weren't advanced enough for either to ask about preferences. She chose the plainest garments in the store and hoped that Lin would like them.

Violet had been raised in the south. She learned to embroider and sew at her nursemaid's knee and knew that something pretty against one's skin made ladies feel beautiful from the inside out. Her own delicates were adorned with ruffles and ribbons. The edges were lacy and embroidered.

Her face grew so warm it was a miracle her head didn't burst into flames right on the spot.

She had been trying to forget it, but the fact remained that when she woke in Mister Harvey's home she had been divested of her clothing and wore a nightdress he had gotten from her own bedroom. That meant he had perhaps undressed and dressed her. She hoped she hadn't been unconscious and uncovered before this man's eyes, but aside from asking she could not know—and she would not ask.

Nonetheless, he had gone for her nightdress, hadn't he? That meant he had been in her drawers—and had seen her drawers and other unmentionables. He knew she did not cotton to plain undergarments any more than a dance hall girl dressed in a miner's hat.

He had seen her underwear.

And he was the only man on the planet who had done so.

If the floor could have opened to swallow her, Violet would have welcomed it.

But it would have served no purpose because humiliation does not die in a heartbeat but, rather, lingers.

Chapter 22

Every once in a while, the fates smile on teachers.

That's what Violet had heard while studying for the profession and it stuck in her mind.

The teaching jackpot came in different guises.

This time, it turned out that she had less than half her pupils show up to the schoolroom. Less than half! In December—it was almost unheard of.

Maybe the unseasonably mild day kept them home. She couldn't blame parents who saw an opportunity to gather family members together to tackle outdoor tasks when the weather cooperated. Most of her pupils were likely busy tending animals, fixing fences, hauling firewood, or making homestead repairs.

Like water runs downstream, luck finds its way to others. Violet decided to be lenient on the day's lessons. Students spent the morning with their readers, but she declared it a day free of arithmetic, history, and recitations at the blackboard. The children were thrilled with the plan. One child declared the day nearly as good as her birthday had been.

After recess, Violet lined the children up by the blackboard in two rows. Taller pupils in the rear, younger and smaller ones in front. She stood back and surveyed the presentation.

"Very good. You all look perfect. I can see every smiling face, and your families will be able to see you all, too."

The holiday custom in Charleston for schoolchildren to put on a Christmas show for family and friends fit right into the Wylder holiday plan. The musicale would take place during the holiday party, right before Santa Claus made an entrance to hand out gifts.

There didn't need to be an extensive program but there had to be something—and so far, the children hadn't practiced even one song.

It was past time—and Violet knew it. Hopefully learning songs on a Friday afternoon made sense. If the children were excited about the show and the music, they would practice over the weekend. They might even teach the songs to some of the children who weren't present today.

Maybe the fates would smile some more on her and the Wylder schoolroom.

"We gotta sing 'Rock-a Bye-Baby' at the program, Miss Bloom," the youngest of the Milligan sisters, Beatie, said. She reminded Violet of own sister, Pansy, so she had a special spot in her teacher's heart. But now, her opinion met refusal.

"No, I don't believe we will. We are going to sing Christmas carols."

A few of the others smiled but Beatie scowled.

"But we gotta. Jesus is gettin' born and havin' a birthday. That's what we sing to babies."

"Let me make you a deal: When it's your birthday, we'll sing that for you but for the Christmas program we'll sing some carols. Trust me, you are going to like the songs I've chosen."

The child didn't look happy, but Violet kept to her

singing lesson. She ignored the disgruntled stare and willful refusal to sing.

Let her stew a bit. She'll come around when she sees what fun the others are having.

"What's a carol?" Owen held a hand up after he spoke. A good boy, but one who had a difficult time following classroom rules. Violet let it go, his speaking out of turn.

"A carol is a song we sing at Christmastime. Sometimes we go from house to house, singing pretty songs for our neighbors. That's called Christmas caroling."

"So we're gonna sing outside?" Owen tilted his head to the side, ignoring the boy standing beside him who laughed at the question. "In the cold? We're settin' to sing in the cold?"

"No, you numbskull—we ain't goin' to be singin' outside. It'll prob'ly be snowin' on Christmas Eve." It was too much for Will to stand quietly by or to let her answer. He had to chime in—which forced her to correct him and issue a reprimand. The other children knew it and stared at the boy, waiting to see what would happen next.

Will knew it, too. He'd been too excited to hold his tongue. Now he'd pay the price for his thoughtlessness—and his use of the word "ain't" in her schoolroom.

"William Hunter, what have I said about calling your classmates names?"

The eleven-year-old met her gaze. "Not to do it, ma'am."

"And what did you call Owen?"

"I called him a numbskull, ma'am."

"Is that his name?"

"No, ma'am."

"And what about the word you used, the one I've corrected you about many times before?"

He crinkled his brows and tipped his head to the side. "Jackass, ma'am?"

"William Hunter! You did not call Owen a jack— you did not say that in my classroom, did you?"

A fast shake of his head sent his long brown hair sliding along his shirt collar. "No, ma'am. I thought you meant this morning, when I called him a jackass—but I ain't done it in the schoolhouse, ma'am." He smiled. "I just done it outside."

While the other pupils learned the words to "Silent Night" Will stood at the chalkboard writing the word "numbskull" one hundred times so he would not forget the unsuitable word had no place in a young man's vocabulary.

Violet tried not to look at Beatie's sullen expression. The child flatly refused to sing, despite having a delightful voice and a genuine fondness for anything musical. Stubbornness kept the child's arms crossed over her chest and the pink lips drawn into a tight line.

When they had practiced a half-dozen times, she passed out sleigh bells on leather straps to six of the children. When she offered one strap to Beatie, the little girl glared at the ceiling so Violet handed it to Owen who beamed as if she'd given him a bagful of mints.

"Now we're going to sing 'Jingle Bells' so we know it in case Santa decides to visit us. He would like to hear it, I'm sure, so let's sing clearly. And those of you with bells, jangle them when I wave my hand like this." She raised her right hand beside her cheek and shook it back and forth. When she did, the jinglers jangled on cue. "Very good. So, let's begin…"

This song elicited more enthusiasm than the first had. Her pupils sang loudly and with so much gusto that by the time they came to the concluding jingling and jangling, everyone was red-faced and smiling.

Except for Beatie, who had focused her gaze on the tips of her shoes.

Violet dismissed the children for the weekend. They dropped their bells on her desk, gathered their belongings, and put on their coats, boots, and cold weather accessories. She bid each farewell at the door.

When one tried to walk past without saying anything, Violet put a hand on her shoulder. "Goodbye, Beatie. I hope you have a pleasant weekend."

A pause. "Goodbye, Miss Bloom. I hope you do, too."

It didn't come close to the typical farewell this child gave her, but it would do.

"I hope you'll sing with us on Monday. I missed hearing your beautiful voice today."

She didn't get a response, but she knew the little one would consider her words. Part of teaching took place outside of the schoolroom, in the lessons the children took away from the things she said, the work they did, and the material she taught. Good teachers travel in their pupils' hearts and minds. Now she hoped that Beatie carried her into the weekend and realized what was meaningful and necessary, and what was not.

Violet stood on the front step for a moment after the children blended into the passersby.

Cowboys, ranch hands, traders, townsfolk, drifters,

miners, strangers, and neighbors filled the busy streets.

A Native dressed in fur and hides, with so many strings of beads hanging from his saddle that he click-clacked every time his horse took a step, passed. She assumed the man traveled to the far side of town where she knew some trading occurred. She would have stopped him right there and bought several lengths of colorful beads to use in her holiday decorations if it were possible. But that would start tongues wagging lickety-split so she contemplated making her own beads. If it were summertime, maybe she could have managed it by letting them dry in the sun but in the dead of winter the endeavor seemed unlikely to be successful.

Shaking her head in dismay, Violet turned to go back inside. She planned to clean the schoolroom as quickly as possible and get on home to see Lin.

"Miss Bloom! A moment of your time, please!"

She turned. Mister Harvey strode toward her. He carried a valise and held the hand of a young girl.

A pretty blonde woman walked beside them.

"Mister Harvey. How nice to see you." Violet clasped her hands at her waist and waited for the trio to come closer.

When they were nearer, she saw that the expensive traveling outfits both females wore looked hand tailored. They each carried a fur muff. Their boots were black leather and even travel dust could not mask their quality.

No doubt they had alighted from the stagecoach. It was Friday, one of the two days of the week when the coach arrived in Wylder.

"Miss Bloom, I want you meet Miss Janet Harvey,

my sister."

Oh, his sister.

The jealous twinge she'd been struck by subsided. Violet smiled and murmured, "Pleased to make your acquaintance, Miss Harvey."

"And yours, Miss Bloom."

He looked from one woman to the other before he met Violet's gaze and said, "And this is my daughter, Alexia. Alexia, say hello to Miss Bloom. She's the schoolteacher in Wylder, so you'll be seeing a lot of her."

The girl had been staring at the snow-covered ground, but she looked up when her father finished speaking. Perhaps twelve or so, with striking hazel eyes and auburn hair, anyone would recognize the child as his by their similar high cheekbones and full lips. The resentful glare did not come from him, however.

"Miss Bloom." The girl's words dripped ice. "Pleased to make your acquaintance. But Father is wrong. I won't be seeing you because I'm not going to this stupid little school in this stupid town. I hate Wylder—and I'm not staying, no matter what my father thinks."

The smile froze on Thomas's handsome face. He leaned nearer the child and said, "Honey, you're being quite rude to Miss Bloom. You're tired from traveling and need to rest. But first, you will apologize."

Alexia met Violet's gaze again. "I'm sorry I was rude to you."

Thomas straightened.

"But I meant what I said—I hate Wylder and I'm going back to Philadelphia as soon as I can. And no one can stop me!"

The girl turned and ran. She dodged two huge horses pulling a wagon and dashed around the corner onto Wylder Street.

No one said a word because, really, what could anyone say to that?

The sparkle left Thomas's eyes. His mouth set in a thin line and his shoulders fell. He looked diminished.

He put his hands on his hips.

Violet dropped her gaze to the pistol he wore. It was a Colt revolver, the same model used by Union soldiers. She had seen a few of the Army model 1860, like this one, when she helped in the hospital. Sometimes a Union soldier would be brought in if his regiment somehow left him behind, and his belongings would be kept with him—except, of course, for his weaponry.

They carried an assortment of rifles but many in the cavalry, artillery, and infantry troops used the Colt 1860.

Violet's gaze lifted. She stood in the presence of a man who had most likely fought in the war for the Union side. The blood of Confederate soldiers was on this man's hands.

She had been in his arms.

His lips had been on hers.

And she had enjoyed both.

Chapter 23

Violet's heart had been heavy since parting from Thomas. The realization of all that he had done in the past, and her growing sentiments for the man, tore at her emotions. She could not allow herself to fall in love with a Union soldier.

The very first shots of the war were fired in Charleston Harbor, near the city of her birth. She owed it to her fellow South Carolinians, every soldier who had fought for the Confederacy, her family, and friends to never forget that fateful April day at Fort Sumter.

She owed it to herself to never forget.

Violet pondered the issue the entire walk home and concluded that she would break her association with the man. She planned to return the book he had gifted her. And despite Wylder's small size, she was going to do her best to avoid seeing him.

Violet went home for the weekend with a surprise for Lin.

Lin also had a surprise to share.

Violet walked into the house and found warmth and light.

Coming home to comfort lifted her spirits. She removed her boots and slipped into the soft leather moccasins she wore indoors. She hung her coat and other outdoor garments on hooks inside the entry door.

She checked her hair in the mirror beside the

hooks. A tendril escaped the tight bun and dangled by her right cheek but otherwise it stayed nearly as neat as it had been when she began the day. The credit for that went to her sister Lily, who had shown her the value of some well-placed hairpins.

Violet tucked the surprise for her new friend underneath her arm and headed for the kitchen. Delicious aromas would have led her there even if her eyes were closed.

Lin stood beside the stove, stirring something in a big pot that smelled so incredible it made Violet's mouth water. Her houseguest hadn't heard her enter. She hummed an exotic melody.

"Lin?"

The Chinese woman whirled around, holding the heavy wooden spoon between them like a weapon. Red sauce dripped onto the floor. When she saw who had come upon her, she plopped the spoon back into the pot and bent to wipe the splotch of sauce with a fingertip. Then she stood, nodded her head, and said, "Hello."

Pronunciation needed work but the greeting was borne on a wide grin.

"Hello. It's so nice to walk in and have a warm house. Thank you for lighting candles. too."

"Candle. Look." She pointed to the candle burning on the table. The candlesticks were in their usual spots but now a piece of glass leaned against the wall behind them. It reflected the flame, increasing the illumination. Where Violet lit two candles, Lin had kindled one. The light in the room glowed even brighter with the mirror than when two candles were lit without it.

"You found that little mirror in the cutlery drawer, didn't you?" She hadn't used it in ages and had forgotten about its existence.

"Is good?" An expression of uncertainty appeared.

"Yes, it's very good! Well done, really. We shall save on candles and have more light than ever. What's not to love about that?"

She didn't believe Lin understood everything she said but it did not matter. Soon her houseguest would comprehend and speak without difficulty. She would read, too.

"I have a surprise for you, as well." Violet handed her the blue McGuffey she had brought home from the schoolhouse. The most elemental reader, ideal for teaching the alphabet, basic vocabulary, and grammar, it provided a foundation for further learning. Once Lin mastered the first book, they would move on to the next.

Violet had often wondered if it were possible to offer English lessons to those who struggled with learning the language. Chinese workers like Lin and her brother, the Arapaho, Cheyenne, and other tribes, and all the other immigrants who worked the mines, railroad, ranches, and more needed to learn. They should understand everything being said to them, and how to respond. Perhaps there would be fewer shootings if there weren't as many misunderstandings.

But that topic would keep for another time. Now, she needed to concentrate on helping Lin.

Lin held it out with a sorrowful gaze. "Thank you. No read English."

She pressed it back toward her friend and nodded. "I know. But I want to teach you English. Then you shall be able to read. Would you like that?"

It had struck her that by offering English Lin might

feel insulted, as if her Chinese weren't worthy or sufficient. Violet hoped she understood the motivation behind the effort to help her learn some skills that would be valuable to someone living in a mostly English-speaking country.

She needn't have worried.

Lin clutched the book to her chest and beamed. It was the most expressive she had been so far, and the sight of her upturned lips, dazzling teeth, and the joy in her gaze brought a smile to Violet's face, too.

"I like very much. I learn English, we talk better."

"Yes, Lin, we shall talk more easily if you speak more English. Although I have to say, you do really well now. I am amazed by how much you already know. Did your brother teach you?"

A sharp nod and a sober shrug. "Yes. He teach. Good brother. Very good man."

"I'm sure he was. And he did a wonderful job teaching you the basics. We will work together to teach you the English your departed brother did not get to."

"Thank you." Lin placed the book on the table beside one of the places she had set. "We eat?"

Violet went to the basin to wash up. "Yes, we eat. Then, we learn some English."

Chapter 24

Saturday morning showed Mother Nature's fickle side. No more calm weather for Wylder. No, Friday's gift had been a singular event. Now, the wind howled, snow fell, and the gray clouds scudding across the sky appeared ominous.

Violet looked out the parlor window as she rubbed her hands up and down her upper arms. Glancing at the inclement weather gave her a chill.

There were Christmas preparations to finalize and if she didn't attend to the details now…well, it wouldn't look good. Letting things slide would give the impression that the upcoming holiday didn't mean much. If there was anything a new schoolteacher wanted to avoid, giving the wrong idea to anyone about anything topped the list. Teaching demanded walking a fine line—propriety and social niceties could elevate her standing in town. One false move, though, could bring ruin. It had happened to many schoolteachers. She couldn't let it happen to her.

Lin adamantly refused to accompany her, which struck Violet as odd.

Her attitude reminded her of Beatie's stubbornness yesterday afternoon about singing.

And that led to her recollecting the meeting with Mister Harvey and his family.

She refused to even think of that man as anything

other than "Mister Harvey" now that she discerned his past. She planned to work at not thinking of him at all.

She could be stubborn, too, when she had a mind to be.

Leaving Lin at home studying the McGuffey Reader, Violet set off for town. The snow made walking a tad slippery, so she watched her footing. She did not wish to end up in another snowbank.

Minnie Milligan and her husband lived with their six children. Beatie was the youngest girl, trailed by three brothers who were too young for school.

Minnie somehow found time to assist whenever a need for help arose in Wylder. How she did it, with all those little ones, no one knew.

Now Brenda, the eldest child, answered the door to their home. Near the railroad tracks, in a less-desirable section of town, it showed a bare-wood exterior. But it had a clean porch and from what Violet could see, it looked immaculate inside, as well.

Brenda jiggled a baby on one hip. The fourteen-year-old hoped to go to teacher's college when she graduated the Wylder School. Violet was helping her figure out ways to finance her schooling—ways that did not include the child doing anything improper.

"Miss Bloom, it's nice to see you. But should you be out on such a morning? You'll catch your death, ma'am."

"It's good to see you, too. But I'm fine. I need a quick word with your mother if she's available."

"Mama's almost finished with the beds. Want to come in while I get her?"

She declined. Her boots were a mess and that gave her a good excuse for not being intrusive. She didn't like to peek closely at her pupils' home lives.

"I'll wait, thank you."

She stood on the porch and looked up at the sky. Unless she got her errands done soon, she would be caught in the weather.

Earlier in the season this part of the territory had been hit with a blizzard. Being from South Carolina, Violet had read about blizzards but had never seen one for herself. Now she would rather not witness another for a long time. Nothing about the blizzard had been good, except watching it end.

The door opened behind her, so she turned and smiled. Minnie Milligan must be nearing thirty, and she looked every bit of those years. She was rail thin, and Violet imagined she sacrificed her own health and nutritional needs for those of her children.

Her hands were red and chapped but she put one out to place on Violet's arm. "Won't you come inside? You must be chilled, standing out here."

"No, thank you. I can't stay. I came by to check on the fare for the Christmas party. Is everything under control? And is there anything you need me to do?"

Missus Milligan had taken charge of the refreshments. That meant she had contacted all the other pupils' mothers and coordinated what every family would bring to the holiday table.

Some of the families whose children attended the Wylder School were barely scraping by so it concerned Violet that they would be pressed into an obligation they could not meet. She wanted every family in town at the celebration, regardless of economic standing. If there were any who could not contribute, she meant to offer a dish in their stead.

"No, nothing at all." The other woman waved a hand in the air between them, as if the whole event were completely under control. "Everyone is bringing a dish to put out. Most will be sweets but there will be some heartier stews and potato dishes, as well."

"Ah…" She wanted to be delicate but needed the truth. "Is every family able to contribute? Comfortably, I mean? I don't want anyone to take food from their tables to bring on Christmas Eve. I don't want families hungry on Christmas Day, you understand."

The other woman nodded, as if she had already considered the same possibilities. "I get what you're sayin', ma'am. Everyone who's bringing something is able to do so. And we have a couple of local folks who contributed to the party, on the side, kind of. I'm planning on using their funds to cover the cost of ingredients for dishes for those who are struggling. And there will be enough left over to make sure those who need it will get a meal for Christmas Day, too."

The news stunned Violet. Wylder was not a wealthy town. Oh, sure, there were those who had money, but most of the people were hard-working, just-making-it folk.

To think some had made it possible for all to be cared for during this yuletide season nearly brought her to tears.

"Well, that is good to know. Remember that if you need anything at all, please send word to me at school. A note with one of the children will do. And thank you, Missus Milligan."

"No trouble at all. My pleasure."

"Well, thank you again." She tucked her scarf up higher on her chin and went for the edge of the porch, one wooden slat up from the snowy street. Before she stepped off, she turned. Minnie Milligan still stood in the partially open doorway.

"Missus Milligan? May I ask who contributed to the Christmas festivities and paid to feed the, ah, less-fortunate families?"

The woman put her head out the door and lowered her voice. "Doc and Mister Harvey. They's the two who gave me money for the school and the families, but both asked I don't let on that they did it. But I don't suppose they meant to keep it from you, since you're the schoolteacher. But it was them—Doc and that nice Mister Harvey."

Chapter 25

The snow let up a bit, although the sky threatened to open again at any time so Violet picked up the pace. There were two other stops on the list, and she wanted to get to both, and then get back home.

She walked past the schoolhouse and church, toward the blacksmith and livery. Seeing the deserted back street between the wagon repair shop and land office, she cut through and walked past the Five Star Saloon.

If it were Saturday evening instead of morning, she never would have taken that route. Saloon clientele could get rowdy, particularly on Friday and Saturday nights. An unescorted female shouldn't walk the back street past midafternoon but on this snowy morning nothing stirred on the short stretch that passed by the side of the saloon.

Relief washed over her when she made it back to Old Cheyenne Road and some distance from the Five Star. Day or night, she didn't feel comfortable being so close to the drinking establishment.

The Union Pacific came through once a week, on Sundays, so tomorrow there would be lots of activity but when Violet passed the train depot it looked tucked in for the day. She stopped to peek at the tracks headed out of town. She had never been past Wylder, although someday she planned to visit Cheyenne. Who could tell? Maybe she would go further than that, even. One could never know about such things.

But today, the second target on her must-do list came into view.

The post office building had been built right beside the telegraph office. They were this side of the railroad tracks.

Past the telegraph office, on the other side of the tracks, stood the Wylder County Social Club. It was more likely she'd see the Pacific Ocean before she got a gander at the inside of the club.

It wasn't that she had anything against the girls or Miss Adelaide. Violet simply did not have any business in a whorehouse. Truth be told, most schoolteachers probably never set foot inside such spots. That opportunity didn't often offer itself up to women who weren't "in the business" of doing what was done inside the walls of the building she now gawked at with open curiosity.

She tipped her head to one side as she examined the front of the building for clues. The occupants of the social club were most likely either resting or primping for the Saturday-night rush. She had no idea if a rush occurred any night of the week, but she imagined there might be. And she guessed at what the women inside were doing because she had no actual knowledge of what kept them busy and staring at the building provided no enlightenment. It all seemed very glamorous and so removed from her own dull life that as she stood in front of the post office, craning her neck and picturing life in the social club, she had a pang of disappointment that she would never know for sure whether any of what she imagined was true.

For the first time in her life, Violet wished she had been born a whore instead of a schoolteacher. Not permanently, but for a day. Maybe two. Or even a month, if it all turned out to be as titillating as she dreamed it might be.

She shook her head and turned away. Dreaming of being something she would never be was a waste of time.

And the sky above told her she didn't have time to squander so she went into the post office, paid her three cents postage, and dropped off her weekly letter to the family back home.

She moved a bit more quickly when she left the post office and went straight up Buckboard Alley. It led past Culpepper's Boarding House.

Violet didn't have business at the boarding house, but it wouldn't hurt to walk past, would it? Her vow to avoid Mister Harvey didn't include sidestepping his sister, who might be boarding at Culpepper's. Likelier, perhaps, that Miss Harvey stayed with her brother, but one never knew. Violet wasn't sure what, if anything, she would say to the woman if she saw her again. But if the other did strike up a conversation, she planned to mention that the Union Pacific came through tomorrow…and led directly out of town, if she and her brother were interested in making their way back to whatever northern hole they'd crawled out of.

Good Lord, whatever am I thinking?

She gave herself a mental shake, passed the boarding house without turning her gaze toward it as punishment for having such a horrid thought, turned right at the corner, and headed down Wylder Street.

Had she been paying attention instead of chastising

herself for her lapse in kindness, she wouldn't have run smack dab into the sheriff.

But she wasn't—so she did.

Thankfully, he grabbed her by the shoulders before she could slip on the snow and ice and disgrace herself.

"Whoa there, Miss Bloom! Easy now, get your feet under you." His thick moustache moved when he smiled down at her. "Wouldn't want our schoolteacher to take a tumble right out here in the middle of the street, would we?"

"Oh, my! How clumsy of me, turning a corner without watching where I was going. I'm sorry, Sheriff. Please forgive me."

He dropped his hands when she steadied herself. The fact that he knew her name came as a surprise, but she supposed a man in his position must know—or know of—all the townsfolk. And those on the homesteads and ranches, as well.

"No clumsiness, and nothing to forgive." He looked up to the darkening sky and then back down to meet her gaze. "I think we'd all be wise to get about our business and go on home. It looks like we're going to get some more snow before the day's out."

"I agree. Pardon me, but I'll be on my way now."

Violet took one step, but the sheriff's words stopped her. The rasp in his voice hinted at countless nights spent breathing in campfire smoke.

"Not so fast, ma'am. Now that we've run into each other, do you mind if I ask you a question? Being in your position, you know many of Wylder's citizens so you might be able to assist me with an investigation. Can you spare a moment, and maybe help me out?"

She couldn't deny his request although she didn't

imagine she could be of any use in an investigation. Unless his search included looking for the McGuffey she had taken from the schoolhouse—and fully intended to return when Lin finished with it—she had no information of a disreputable sort.

"Of course. I'm happy to help if I can."

"Good to hear." He took a step toward her and closed the gap she had made when she tried to walk away. The lawman limped, as if his knees pained him. He fixed his probing gaze on her. "I'm looking for a woman who seems to have gone missing. I wonder if you know of any such person. Perhaps one of your pupils mentioned a lady showing up suddenly in an unusual place?"

"My pupils? No, I haven't heard any of them mention anyone—man or woman—who appeared unexpectedly."

The sheriff ran a slow hand over his beard. "Maybe you know of a woman who seems out of place, then. This woman who disappeared, she's a Chinese lady. I need to find her and speak with her, that's all. Have you heard any of the other ladies in town mention such a person—a Chinese woman who seems to be without a place to stay?"

Her blood ran cold. "No, sir. None of the women have mentioned anyone like that to me."

He touched the brim of his worn hat. "Thank you, Miss Bloom. I appreciate your taking the time to speak with me. Now get home safely, you hear? Storm's coming and you don't want to be caught out in it."

"Will do, Sheriff. But I'm curious…can you tell me why you want to question the woman?"

He tucked his thumbs in his belt loops and rocked

back on his heels.

"Won't do no harm to satisfy your curiosity, ma'am. Chinese woman's wanted for questioning in connection with a death. Her brother was killed. The ones who killed him, they say he had something that belonged to them and when they demanded he return it, he tried to shoot them. So I got a case of self-defense, a missing Chinese lady, and property that ain't been found."

She tried to hide her amazement by asking a final question, the way she thought an interested but completely uninvolved person might do. "How awful. Whatever did the man have that would cause such an unfortunate outcome?"

"Well, I'm told it's a very large, valuable black pearl."

Chapter 26

"Why, it is a good thing, indeed, to see you up and about." Gertie strode across the floorboards inside the mercantile like a battleship heading out to war. She didn't look in either direction, targeting Violet and not slowing until she reached her side. "Let me get a good look at you. Why, you're a slip of a woman, aren't you? It's tricky to tell the truth of a person when they're in their nightclothes, now isn't it?"

Violet wished the other would keep her voice down. She didn't need to be at the top of the town gossip chain and if Gertie continued this way there would be no stopping it.

She tried to lead by example, replying in a soft tone and attempting to steer the conversation into more favorable waters. "How nice to see you again—and on such a cold, miserable morning. I hope your errands don't keep you out in the weather too long."

"I had to pop in for a few things. You know, with Christmas coming and all, I thought to prepare. I'm signed on to bring my pumpkin bread, made from my granny's recipe, to the Christmas Eve party. It's wise to get some molasses before everyone decides they need it. I know this is your first winter here, so you aren't aware, but we sometimes have shortages. When the wagons can't get through or the deliveries don't make it onto the trains, we make do with what we have."

"I'm from South Carolina. I lived through shortages during the war and we southerners are familiar with making do."

"Well, that will be in your favor out here in the west, dear. But more to the point, how are you? You look well, if a bit peaked."

If she had left her assessment at "well" Violet's feathers wouldn't be ruffled. But the woman added "peaked"—unnecessarily, in her eyes. It stretched her already taut nerves even tighter.

"I am quite recovered." She felt Mother's long-distance poke, a reminder to maintain her manners at all times so she added, "Thank you for helping me when I found myself under the weather."

"Oh, no problem at all. That's what we do here in Wylder. We look after each other."

"So I've heard."

"Hearing—that reminds me, were you overly frightened by the roostered-up no-gooders looking to raise a ruckus stampeding through the streets the other morning? Weren't much before sunrise, you'd have to be dead to not have heard 'em."

"I heard them. And, no, I didn't become too alarmed. I guess things like that, a little bit of noise and such, are part of living out here. I know I'm not in Charleston anymore."

"You're a wise one, you are. No, you're not in the old states now and things are different in these parts."

Violet had come in for one item and wished she hadn't bothered. Surely, she could have done well with whatever she had in the pantry. Lin might like some coffee, though. They were going to have a discussion when she got home, and they might need something stronger than tea.

She reached for a tin of Arbuckle's Coffee and tried to make a graceful exit.

"Yes, well, so very nice to see you again. I'll look forward to tasting your grandmother's pumpkin bread at the party." She shot Gertie a smile and gave a polite nod. Mother would be proud if she could see her now. "I must be on my way. I want to get home before the snow starts up again."

"Yes, that's a good idea. You don't need any extra chilling on them bird bones of yours."

"Good day, Gertie."

While she kept her smile in place, she fumed inwardly. Why on earth did folks think it essential to add observations on her body, mind, health—or anything else? She had no idea that when she became a schoolteacher, she would be the subject of so many opinions. Had she known, she may have begged Father to allow her to become an undertaker. At least undertakers didn't have to deal with people shooting their mouths off the way teachers did.

She squeezed her eyes closed for a fast second and sucked in a deep breath. If she let every person in this town get under her skin, she would lose her mind. The sooner she got used to the way things were done in Wylder, the better it would be for her.

Violet headed for the counter so she could pay for the coffee and get out of the store. She needed air, and some peaceful moments, and she surely wouldn't get them here.

Her haste was, once again, her downfall.

She hurried in the snowstorm on Monday.

Threw convention to the wind and kissed a man

she had just met.

Then rushed to bring Lin into her home and perhaps harbored a murderer and jewel thief.

She ran into the sheriff while entertaining less-than-kind notions about someone she didn't even know.

And now she practically bowled over the one person in town she wanted to avoid, all because she rushed without bothering to watch her step.

"Miss Bloom! Pardon me, but I came close to knocking you off your feet."

Mister Harvey reached out to help steady her, but she backed away. She would not abide that man's hands on her ever again.

Her backside collided with a checkerboard set on a barrel at the end of the aisle near the pot-belly stove. The wooden checkers fell to the floor and scattered.

"Oh!" Violet knelt to grab at a red checker that rolled across the floorboards. She snatched it before it disappeared between the stove's black legs. There were a few more near the fire so she collected them before she stood up. She returned them to the board which had tilted far enough to tip the checkers off but remained in place on the barrel top.

"I believe we got them all." His hand came close to touching hers when he placed his stack of checkers beside those she gathered. The wooden circles made a slight clacking noise when they hit each other.

She pulled her hand back, put it on her midsection and murmured, "Thank you."

Violet walked to the counter, determined not to let anything get in her way of leaving. She placed her Arbuckle's down and reached for her change purse. Mister Wylder wrapped the coffee tin in brown paper and tied it with string from the spool hanging above the counter for that purpose. She handed her money over, thanked the shop owner, and tucked the package beneath one arm.

"Miss Bloom? I hoped to speak with you."

His words sent her mind into a tangle. If it wouldn't have caused a flap, she would have ignored the man.

She did not turn around but looked over her shoulder at him. He lingered by the counter. A small pile of goods sat on the wooden countertop while their prices were tallied on a slip of brown paper.

"I am in a hurry."

"But it's not personal. It's about your schoolhouse." His voice took on a no-nonsense tone that made it clear he meant to have this discussion, whether she wanted it or not. "About a new pupil, that is."

She considered her options. Gertie most likely eavesdropped, Finn Wylder couldn't help but hear the discussion while he tallied, and who knew how many others lurked in the aisles behind them. Her reply must be ladylike and not raise any suspicions regarding her true feelings for the man.

Damned social graces.

"That seems to be a matter to discuss at the schoolhouse. Not here."

"My daughter and I will be at the schoolhouse early Monday morning to discuss her enrollment. I trust you will have time to speak with me then, Miss Bloom."

Annoyance came through with every word, but she refused to let him intimidate her.

"Any parent who appears in my schoolroom during school hours has my full attention. Good day, Mister Harvey."

She lifted her chin and headed for the door, mindful of keeping her spine straight. She did not look over her shoulder, but felt his glare burning a hole in the back of her head.

As she passed the notice board near the entrance, her gaze raked across the scraps of paper tacked to it. Locals and businesses advertised items either up for sale or, in some cases, needed. Additionally, it provided a public spot for bounty hunters and law officials to display their notices.

A rectangular poster tacked to the bottom right-hand corner of the board stopped her dead.

Beneath the bold-faced word "WANTED" was an artistic rendering of Sun Lin.

There were smaller words at the bottom of the notice, but Violet didn't bother to read them. She peeked over her shoulder, saw the others were engaged in business at the counter, and reached for the poster.

The crinkling sound as she tore the paper from its spot and curled it in her fist was hardly discernable. She opened the door with her free hand and stepped outside.

No one could see her gasp for air as she turned toward home.

No one, that is, except the Chinese man who followed her.

Chapter 27

Violet wanted to get home.

No more stopping to speak with townsfolk. No more errands.

Just home.

And because the commotion invading her mind and the acid churning in her gut were complete distractions, she failed to notice the man who came up behind her. Not until he knocked her off her feet onto the slippery road and tore her reticule from her wrist was she at all aware of his existence.

Thankfully, her skirts offered some padding but when her knees slammed to the ground, her teeth clamped down and caught the side of her tongue between her molars. The coppery taste of blood filled Violet's mouth.

The package of coffee fell into the snow when her arms went out to break the fall. Gloves kept her hands from being scraped on the ice. The left palm hit down squarely but the right hand still clutched the Wanted poster, and it did not land well.

Pain shot up her arm in a burst of white-hot agony. She didn't realize she screamed until she heard it. When she couldn't swallow, she spat bright red blood onto the snow.

Her fall caused a commotion on the street. Those who saw it pointed and hollered. A few men gave chase, going after the man who had knocked her down.

Violet had noticed the small building with a sign above its front window that read "Gemstones," but she had never been inside the establishment. She fell directly in front of its door. Had it been summertime and the door propped open, she would have landed almost in the shop itself.

The door opened and a Chinese man hurried to her aid.

"Oh, no! I saw the man who did this—I saw him walk up behind you, but I could not stop him. I am so sorry, missy. So very sorry." He knelt before her and looked into her eyes. He stared into the right one, then the left, then met her gaze. "You see me good? No problems?"

She opened her mouth to speak but it was filled with blood, so she nodded.

"Here, I help you up. You sit in my shop. We call Doc Coyote." People had gathered so he spoke to the small crowd. "Someone fetch the doctor, please? For the lady?"

He helped her to her feet.

Violet winced when she tried to move her right arm. It throbbed so relentlessly it felt as if it were being stomped on by a dancing bull. She had never seen a bull dance, but it must feel this way.

"Arm hurt? I saw, you fell hard on the arm."

She nodded. The blood trickling down her throat made her nauseated. She hoped she wouldn't embarrass herself by losing the contents of her stomach in this nice man's shop.

A jumble of brightly colored gemstones scattered across the brown leather blotter on a battered wooden desk that occupied a rear corner of the shop were the only signs of disarray. Two dark wooden chairs flanked a belly stove. A circular rug covered most of the pine floorboards. The tiny shop reminded her of its owner, compact and orderly.

The man helped her sit on one of the chairs. He searched her gaze again and must have liked what he saw because he held a hand up, took a cup from a side table, and went outside. He returned almost instantly with a cup of clean snow.

"Here. You put in mouth to stop bleeding."

Violet took it with her good hand and tilted a mouthful of snow between her lips. The chill on her tongue dulled the pain. She held the snow in her mouth until it melted. Then, she swallowed.

"More. It will be good to have more." He smiled encouragingly, motioning with his hand that she should tip the cup into her mouth again. Then he must have realized they hadn't been introduced because he sat in the other chair and put a hand on his chest. "I am Liu Wei. This is my shop. You are welcome here."

His foreign mannerisms and unparalleled courtesy gave him such an air of refinement that she felt as if she were in the presence of an elder. Violet guessed he must be in his late twenties. Medium height, slender build, beautiful skin, long black hair tied in a braid, and deep brown eyes made him very appealing. If she were a woman who found herself attracted to men from China, she might have thought him handsome.

She allowed the melted snow to slide down her throat. Wiggling her tongue about a bit, she sighed when she didn't taste new blood.

Violet took a chance and spoke. "Thank you for

helping me. I am Violet Bloom."

"The schoolteacher. Yes, I know this to be true."

The pain in her arm made it almost impossible to speak without crying. She pulled the injured limb against her coat, hoping that holding it close would help, but it made things worse.

"Your arm. May I see?" When she raised her eyebrows in response he said, "Doctor may be a while. I have some training in medicine. Maybe I can help."

When she nodded, he eased her out of her coat. The paper she had torn from the mercantile board was still crumpled in her hand, so she put it in her coat pocket.

The Chinese man pantomimed rolling up a sleeve, so Violet did so.

He reached out and ran a gentle hand over her forearm. When he reached a spot a few inches above her wrist, she gasped.

"As I thought." He pressed gently. "Sorry to hurt you. I know it is painful. I think you cracked that bone, the one that goes from here—" He touched her wrist with a fingertip. "—to here." He tapped her elbow with the same fingertip.

"I haven't broken a bone before. I had no idea how much it hurts." She hugged her arm to her chest. "Are you sure, Mister Liu?"

He quirked a brow when she addressed him. "I am, yes. In Beijing I had a medical office. I study medicine and I believe you have cracked that arm bone. No worry, though. It will mend. Most bones do heal if we allow them to rest."

While he spoke, he went to a cabinet at the back of the shop. He rummaged around inside before pulling out a beautiful piece of fabric. He opened it up and began to fold it as he walked over. The material looked expensive. It had a light blue background with deep sapphire, amethyst, and crimson figures embroidered onto the weave.

He held up the stunning piece of needlework. The figures were dragons, flying across the sky-blue background.

"That is beautiful."

"If you do not mind, I will wrap your arm. Tightly, so it will mend."

"Oh, no, I couldn't let you do that. I've already caused too much trouble—I can never repay you for your kindness."

He knelt in front of her and placed the folded material on her lap, motioning for her to lay the arm on the fabric. Violet complied, feeling as safe with this man as with the doctor in Charleston she'd known her whole life.

His words touched her heart. "No need to repay. We are humans, all of us, on this earth to serve each other. I help you. Maybe someday you help me. Or if not me, maybe someday you help someone else. It is, like this bandage, the form that holds us together."

Her arm still pained her, but it did not throb so terribly once he had it wrapped.

The door opened and Doc Sullivan entered the shop. He removed his hat and looked at the scene. Then he smiled. "There you go again, Wei, stealing my patients from me."

The Chinese man stood and shook his head. "No need to steal this one. She fell right into my shop."

Chapter 28

Violet could have dropped in place by the time she walked in the front door.

But dropping wasn't an option.

First, she had to deal with Lin. She could not put off having the discussion.

She slipped out of her coat and hung it on the hook inside the door. Unwinding her scarf and removing her hat required one functional hand, and taking the glove off her left went smoothly when she bit the fingertips and tugged. The bare, swollen right hand stuck out of the sling.

The boots were a task she would have preferred not to undertake. The small black buttons took ages to unfasten one-handedly but eventually she got her feet out of them and into her house moccasins.

A nap would have gone over well, but it would have to wait.

Lin sat at the kitchen table, so engrossed in the McGuffey reader that she didn't look up when Violet walked into the room.

"Your concentration skills are admirable."

The woman raised her gaze with a smile on her face. It froze there when she saw the wrapped arm, swollen hand, and trace of blood on Violet's chin.

"You hurt? How? How you hurt?" Lin stood and put her hands out as if to help her friend, but she let them fall. "Where? Where to touch so I don't hurt you?"

"It's fine." She dropped into the chair that Lin pulled away from the table for her. When her guest went to the stove and put the kettle on, she didn't protest. A nice cup of tea would be soothing. Funny, how a cup of water that had leaves soaking in it made such a difference in one's outlook.

Violet waited until Lin served tea. When both cups were poured and she had declined a biscuit with jam, she held a hand out to the vacant chair.

"Lin, please sit. We need to talk."

Her guest's eyes grew more guarded than they were under normal conditions. Violet noticed her lower lip quivered before she pulled herself together. Lin sat and folded her hands on the table. The posture showed she had grown accustomed to hearing unpleasant news.

Violet took a deep breath and sighed it out. She reached her left hand into her skirt pocket and removed the piece of paper. She handed it across the table and watched the other woman uncrumple it.

Lin stared down at the likeness. The artist had probably been given a verbal description and had drawn from that. The product looked enough like Lin that even though she could not read the English words on the poster, she saw the truth of it.

"That's a Wanted poster. I took it off the board at the mercantile. Do you know what a Wanted poster is?"

Lin closed her eyes for a long moment. She opened them, met Violet's gaze, and nodded.

"Yes, I know."

"Do you know why you're being sought by the sheriff?"

Another nod.

"So you know you're wanted for murder? And you didn't tell me?"

Lin's forehead wrinkled and her eyes narrowed. She dipped her chin to her chest. Then her eyes widened, and she shook her head so hard her braid whipped over her shoulder. "No! No—no murder! No, not me."

She believed her. The thought that she would murder someone, especially her own brother, hadn't set well with Violet. But she'd had to see what kind of response the accusation brought. Lin's innocent eyes told the story.

But why, then, did she not seem surprised by the Wanted poster? Lin accepted it, almost as if she expected to be found out...but about what?

"This poster says you're wanted in connection with the murder of Sun Zhiang. Do you know that person?"

"Zhiang my brother."

"Did you kill him?"

"No. I no kill—he my brother!" A tear slid down Lin's cheek. "I no kill."

Violet could not bear the grief in the other's eyes. She went on in a gentler tone. "Do you know who killed your brother?"

Nodding, Lin answered, "Bad man. Very bad man."

"Do you know what he looks like?"

When Lin hesitated, Violet saw fear in her expression. "You need to trust me. I can't help you if you don't trust me."

A sip of tea for each of them, and a few moments to find strength for the one who would need it most.

Violet could tell the story Lin prepared to relate—because in her heart she felt they were close enough that she would confide in her—would not be pretty.

Then Lin began to speak, and Violet had a difficult time keeping from asking her to stop. The horrors were overwhelming, and much worse than she feared.

Chapter 29

Lin didn't need to have a huge command of English to tell her story. Where she could not formulate a word or phrase, she acted out the omission. Her tale was clear, concise, and bone-chilling.

"Sun Lin not my name—not real name." She paused, searched for a word, then went on. "Not whole name. I am Jiang Ying Yue. Sun Lin is name from baby times. Brother not Sun Zhiang—is also childhood name. Brother Jiang Feng Mian. We come from China, from Sichuan, where the giant Buddha resides. Sent by grandfather, sent against our...wants..."

"Against your will? Your grandfather sent you here against your will?"

She nodded. "Yes, that is it. To California. Grandfather think we be safe so far away. But California not safe. We come here. Think we be safe here. But not safe here. Not safe anywhere." Lin's words were low and spoken with so much sorrow.

"Is that why you were disguised as a man? Why you pretended to be two men, you and your brother?"

"Yes. We think maybe no one look for two men. One man and one woman, yes. But two men? No." She sighed, and it sounded pulled all the way from her feet. "But we wrong. They find us. Again, they find us."

Violet could not imagine what it felt like to be pursued the way these siblings had been. And she couldn't fathom why their family sent them so far from home—alone, no less. It made her angry, knowing they went into a new place with little language skills, with great danger following their every move.

"Who found you?"

A shrug. "The bad men. They find us. They kill brother. Now they try to kill me."

There had to be something missing so Violet tried to get the story back to its roots. Father always said that a tree didn't grow from the branches, but from the roots. Want to find out how something got to its present state, check beneath the surface.

"Why did your grandfather send you and your brother from China? Why send you across the world?"

Lin looked at her as if she were feeble-minded. "To keep alive. To save us."

"Where are your parents? Why your grandfather?"

"Parents dead."

"I'm sorry. What did your grandfather try to save you from, Lin?"

"Chinese curse. It say when last Jiang dead, riches of family belong to opposing family. I last. Grandfather killed after he send us on boat. We hear from others. Railroad workers like us."

They heard about their family all the way from China? Those were some deep roots. The riches must be substantial, for one family to send someone to murder another family's last surviving members.

"We have to go to the sheriff. He will help you."

Lin shook her head. "No one can help. Jade burial piece in my possession. They want but I not give. Not their ancestor, they do not deserve."

A Chinese man had knocked her down and stolen

her reticule. Could it be possible he believed she had this jade thingamabob?

"How big is the jade that you have?"

"Not big. Fit in burial suit near chin. Right above heart of princess." She reached inside the neckline of her dress. Her fingers emerged holding a small jade square dangling from a silver chain. It appeared centuries old and although Violet knew nothing at all about jade, she recognized it as priceless. It shone with a luster that made it nearly iridescent.

She leaned closer to see better and noticed something carved near one corner of the small square. "Are those letters? What does it say?"

Lin tucked the piece back inside her clothing. She gave it a pat where it must hang above her heart. "Ying Yue. Name of princess wearing burial suit."

Violet's heart stuttered in her chest. "But…isn't that your name, too?"

A nod. "I am Jiang Ying Yue."

"Are you a princess, too?" She had to ask the question because right now the notion did not seem out of the realm of possibility.

"I am the last princess."

Chapter 30

A sharp rapping came at the door. They shot up from their seats and looked at each other in terrified silence.

Violet grabbed Lin's wrist with her good hand, ran for the far side of the kitchen, and nodded to a small, rectangular door. The pantry cupboard utilized the space beneath the staircase. It wasn't huge but neither was Lin.

Lin unlatched the door, bent low so as not to smack her head on the doorframe, and slipped inside. She crouched beside a bushel of potatoes and stared out with unconcealed fear.

Putting a finger over her lips, and wishing it weren't as dark as the devil's armpit in the cupboard, Violet closed the door. She dropped the latch in place, sealing her friend inside.

They had spent too much time hiding in closets and cupboards this week for her liking. But they would continue to do whatever it took to stay alive.

The rapping sounded again, sharper now. As she went to open the door, she patted her dress pocket with her right hand, sending a spear of pain up to her shoulder. She would never be able to use that hand to her advantage, so she reached over with her left and took the Remington Model 95 from her pocket.

Placing the over-under double-barrel pistol in her

left skirt pocket, she covered the last few feet to the entrance. She did not have heaps of experience shooting left-handed but if it were necessary to protect them, she would manage.

The door opened inward, so she peeked out of the window beside it before she touched the latch.

When she saw Thomas Harvey on her front porch, she considered ignoring his presence. However, the look on his face gave the impression that if she did not open the door, he would continue to rap on it. Or worse. She didn't put it past him to force his way in.

As he lifted his hand to hammer on the wood again, she opened up. His hand stopped inches from her face.

They stood glaring at each other for a long moment before he dropped his hand.

She wanted to get the high ground from the very beginning of this exchange. It didn't matter why he had appeared on her doorstep—she didn't care.

He has to leave—now.

She couldn't say that the man no longer affected her. If anything, her visceral attraction to his nearness had rather increased. Mother told her daughters that yearning for what they could never have was futile, a human condition which often rendered the one who yearned unable to think clearly. Finally, she understood her mother's warning on the topic.

Fortunately, she had learned from Father, as well. He advised that it was wiser to follow logic than emotion. Her traitorous heart had no chance of swaying her mind on this one. She would follow advice from both parents now.

The man who stared down at her with an intensity fierce enough to cow a less-determined woman cleared his throat. His gaze dropped and when he saw her arm, his forehead creased.

"What happened to your arm?"

No idle chitchat, just straight to the point. Ordinarily she liked that about a person but in this circumstance, it peeved her. How did he presume to ask questions that were none of his business?

"I don't believe that's any concern of yours. If that's all you have to say, I'll bid you good day."

Violet tried to swing the door closed but he reached out and put a palm against the wood.

"What is going on? Why are you so ornery all of a sudden?" He did not hide his irritation. "I swear, you confound me. One minute, honey drips from your sweet lips and the next you cut me in half with your icy stare. Would you at least tell me what happened to turn you into a snow queen?"

The long morning had left her tired, overwhelmed, and in pain. On a good day she might have more patience with his temper, but this was not a good day.

"How dare you insult me?"

"You've turned against me and I don't understand why. You're the one who's been insulting. Why, you won't even speak with me when I see you in town. Blast it—do you know what kind of grilling I got from Gertie after you stormed from the mercantile? You made me look foolish."

"No one can make another 'look' anything, Mister Harvey. You look foolish? Well, maybe you should consider that you might *be* foolish."

Southern charm for this man had taken the train out of town yesterday. She had no remorse about being unkind to him. She had not forgotten how he helped her, or how he saved her life more than once, but she didn't owe him anything. That debt had been paid already with Confederate blood.

He could go to Hell for all she cared.

The lie hurt her heart but eventually she might believe it. When she could do so, she would be better off so she planned to repeat the falsehood as often as necessary.

"Perhaps you should consider how you look right now, Miss Bloom."

"I don't care one bit how I look to you. Are you finished here?"

She went to close the door, but he repeated what he had done a few minutes earlier. This time he kept his hand on the wood and held it open.

"Tell me why you're different." He lost the combative tone. He practically begged to comprehend what had changed.

She did not owe him anything but acting with disregard for another went against her disposition. She could give him the truth.

"You fought for the Union, didn't you?"

He narrowed his gaze. "What does that have to do with anything?"

"Answer the question, Mister Harvey. Or don't, it's up to you. But I know a Union sidearm when I see one. And your family is from back east—the northeast, to be exact. Two and two make four. I know what you are."

He shook his head in disbelief. "The war has been over for longer than a decade. And you couldn't have been more than a child when it occurred. How can you still think any of that has any bearing on what we do here, or who we are?"

"I saw more than any child should see, and at right about the same age your daughter is now. I witnessed what the Union soldiers did—and I have not forgotten. I will not forget, I assure you."

"Hasn't anyone ever told you not to hold a grudge? I didn't want to consider it, but I see that you really do cling to what is best forgotten."

She shook her head. "I know what I know. As I said, two plus two makes four—and in this case, adding up your sums does not earn you a passing grade."

"You should check your arithmetic." He took his hand off the door and plowed it through his hair. Then he smashed his Stetson back onto his head and turned.

She did not watch him walk away.

Convincing her heart to harden itself against the man would be challenging, but necessary. Hopefully, it would not prove to be impossible.

Chapter 31

Violet leaned against the closed front door and took a deep, shuddering breath.

She had not been raised to be mean to anyone. Neither she nor her three sisters would have ever dreamed of speaking a harsh word or intentionally choosing to hurt someone. She had to draw from the deepest part of herself to act rudely toward Thomas, but she knew it must be done.

No, that wasn't true. She didn't know anything in this moment but didn't see how it would benefit either of them to continue the association. Better to end things right here, before they became further entangled.

She couldn't ponder over any of it.

A princess in her pantry waited to be released.

Violet took two steps toward the kitchen before a knock sounded on the front door.

Could he really be back?

She turned and yanked the door open, ready to deliver an angry barrage of words designed to remove him from her life forever. Fortunately, she did not begin to speak before opening the door.

Sheriff Hanson removed his black hat when he saw her. "Miss Bloom."

She glanced behind him. Gloom and a darkening sky—but no sign of the man who had recently departed.

Her gaze fell on the badge pinned to the lapel of his

worn black coat, then rose to meet blue eyes that hinted he'd seen just about everything a man could see. Lines ran from the corners of his eyes and creases etched his forehead, but they added to his rugged appeal.

Violet guessed him to be in his late fifties. Had he been younger, and she not already battling with a lost heart, he would have been welcome to linger on her doorstep. Instead, she searched for a way to hurry him along.

"Sheriff. I didn't, ah, well I'm a bit surprised to see you. Is anything wrong over at the schoolhouse?" One of her biggest fears, that someone would damage that precious building and Wylder would lose the school, sent her pulse racing.

"No, nothing like that, ma'am. I don't mean to startle you, but this isn't about the schoolhouse." He paused, as if waiting for her to invite him in. When she didn't, he put a hand in his pocket and pulled out her reticule. "I know you were accosted on Wylder Street, and I am truly sorry for that. It seems that the holidays can bring out the worst in folks sometimes."

She took the torn, dirty item from him with her left hand.

"The holidays? Why, I would think that this time of year would encourage kindness and goodwill." She could not tell him she suspected she had been targeted because of the Chinese connection. "Why ever would someone do this to another during this festive season? I don't understand."

The sheriff twirled his hat in his hands. "Well, it's like this: People can be hard-pressed for money during the holidays. Winter can be lean times, even without the added cost of festivities. One desperate moment can turn a law-abiding citizen into a miscreant. I think that's what happened here."

He made good points. His law enforcement expertise showed how the criminal mind worked.

She wanted to ask him about how to deal with assassins but of course she could not.

"Yes, well you're probably correct. It's unfortunate that folks would do such things, but I see how it happens."

"I didn't find your bag. A girl, I believe the eldest Milligan child, found it. She brought it home to her mother and her mother brought it to me. The Milligan girl seemed certain it belongs to you. Then I heard from Doc that you were assaulted and lost your property, so I put it all together and came right over."

Her free-spirited sister, Daisy, had received the reticule as a gift and thought it too "fussy" so she passed it on to Violet, who had been grateful to receive it.

It reminded her of Daisy. Amazing how small things could cover so many miles in an instant.

"I am thankful for your kindness. And I will show my gratitude to Missus Milligan and her daughter, as well."

The sheriff put his hat on. He looked down at her arm and gave his head a slow, sad shake. "You take care, Miss Bloom. I hate to see anyone hurt in Wylder. I am sorry for what happened this morning. Hopefully tomorrow will be better."

Her arm hurt, her heart hurt, and she felt tuckered out emotionally, physically, and spiritually, but she managed a nod.

"Thank you, Sheriff. Good day."

This time when she shut the door, she locked it. It didn't matter who came calling, she wasn't letting them in. She'd done enough socializing for one day already.

Chapter 32

With two days left before the Christmas party, Violet had no time to waste.

Sunday morning brought more menacing gray clouds. Four inches of new snow had fallen overnight. The dazzling whiteness of the streets showed in sharp contrast to the dark sky. In between, buildings looked frosted.

The ideal day to stoke the fire, brew endless pots of tea, and settle in with heaps of interesting reading material presented itself. A relaxing time for rest and perhaps an afternoon nap, followed by a hearty meal and even more lying about.

If only.

While it sounded idyllic in her head the reality that there were endless tasks to be completed before Christmas carried more weight than lounging. And with one less-able limb, attending to it all posed a challenge.

Damn it.

Violet chuckled. What would Father think if he could read her mind and hear that swear word spoken so forcefully—albeit silently? He would have a proper fit, is what would happen. And he'd surely not hesitate to tell her exactly what was on *his* mind, hearing his daughter use such unladylike language.

Lin came into the parlor carrying a tea tray. She put it on the tea table and poured cups for each of them.

Placing Violet's on the side table beside her chair and within reach of the uninjured left hand, she smiled and asked, "I hear laugh. You happy today?"

"I suppose I am content. Well, about some things. About others? Not so much, but I'm hoping that passes. It has to, doesn't it? After all, I'm not giving it any other choice but to pass—I shall wait and see, I suppose. That is the right thing to do, don't you think?" She ended with a long, drawn-out sigh.

Her companion's eyes grew so huge on her pretty face that she looked like one of the cartoon drawings that had begun appearing in the weekly newspaper.

"This means happy?"

"Oh, I'm sorry, Lin. It's all extremely complicated. But you heard me chuckle, I think. It is almost like laughter, but more of a derisive sound, really. Oh, right. You probably are stuck on that word, aren't you? Derisive…ah, that means cynical or mocking or…well, never mind, it's not important." She realized she spoke in circles, so she paused, took a breath, and smiled. "I apologize. I think out loud and sometimes that can be a bit, well, off-putting."

Hoping to stem the tide of the conversation, Violet reached for her cup and took a sip. Lin's expertise at tea brewing made every teatime a remarkably pleasant experience.

Violet still hadn't been able to address her new friend by her real name. She was used to calling her "Lin" already, and it wouldn't do to take any chances. Revealing the princess's true identity could be the worst mistake either of them might ever make. They could end up dead if the wrong person found out who hid in Violet's home.

They couldn't behave like scaredy cats, either.

Lin's health would suffer in captivity. Everyone benefited from fresh air—even cold, nose-numbing air. And sunshine, too—but that likely wouldn't arrive for weeks to come.

They both needed to get out. As tempting as lying about sounded, Violet knew it served no good purpose. Mother would say that avoiding the inevitable made it worse. Hiding at home, trying to keep out of sight of every Wylder resident because of her fear she might run into one certain man was nonsense.

"Lin, how do you feel about going to the schoolhouse to help me with Christmas preparations this morning?" Lin looked skeptical so she added, "We shall disguise you so no one will ever guess who you are. And if we are asked, we shall say you are a dear friend from back home in South Carolina. Yes, that will do nicely."

Lin raised her eyebrows. She took a sip of tea. Then, a strangled giggle escaped her lips.

"Me? Carolina?" Another choked giggle.

"Yes, South Carolina. No one will be any the wiser if I do all the talking and you stand beside me and show that pretty smile of yours." She made a mental note to clothe Lin in the smallest dress she had, the one tucked in the back of her closet waiting for its seams to be let out. "And by the way, I do believe you just chuckled."

Chapter 33

Before Christmas Eve a case of nerves came over Violet.

She had been so calm, organized, and confident that she had everything under control, but suddenly the jitters hit hard and fast, and she wondered if she had time to catch the Union Pacific out of town. Hop the train and chug off into the sunset, never to be heard of again. Stranger things had happened and would happen again, certainly.

But the absurd notion passed as quickly as her fear.

Violet intended to put on the most wonderful Christmas celebration, one so incredible that folks in Wylder would still talk about it in July.

Lin had finished all the pinecone decorations, so they were going to hang them from the paper garlands the children had assembled. They would swag them from corner to corner, making the schoolroom look magical.

When she devised the plan of hanging the garlands, Violet hadn't had an injured arm. Now she struggled, holding one end of a paper chain up near the ceiling while standing on a chair while Lin stood on another chair holding the other end ten feet away. It seemed unlikely that they would get this accomplished without falling onto their heads or tearing the garlands to shreds.

Hammering tiny nails into the walls to hold the swags with one hand proved impossible, so Lin attempted the feat. Chinese women, including the one currently wielding a hammer, weren't known for being statuesque.

"Wait a minute. Let's look at this again, Lin." Violet stepped down off the chair, placed the garland on the floor, and stood back. "I don't see how we are going to get this done. We may need to make a new plan, although I hate to give up on this one. The paper chains and pinecones will be so festive—if we can hang them."

Lin climbed down and put her hands on her hips. "Too short. Need tallness."

"Yes, you're right. We need tallness here."

They had more work to do, but the garlands were the most important part of decorating left undone. The smaller tasks weren't as essential—and not nearly as obvious. The garlands and tree were the things that everyone would notice when they walked in, and Violet wanted them to be magnificent.

One of the fathers of a pupil delivered a spruce tree to the schoolroom yesterday. He had set it in a pail and placed it in a corner. Tomorrow the children would decorate it. Tuesday, prior to the arrival of the townspeople, she would place small white candles on the branches and light them.

A knock sounded on the front door. Being Sunday morning, she didn't expect anyone, so they turned to each other in surprise.

Violet looked at the belly stove. She and Lin had filled it with wood and opened the vent.

"We started the fire so there's probably a curl of

smoke showing from the chimney, that's all." She walked toward the door while she reassured Lin. "Surely someone is coming to check, to make sure the schoolhouse is secure. There's no need to be concerned."

The other woman gripped the hammer at her side. "Bad men. Remember, bad men."

Violet paused. Lin had a good point. She couldn't assume the assassins hadn't caught up to them. She tiptoed to the door and peeked out the peephole.

Chinese assassins had not come calling.

The man on the steps bent to peer into the tiny hole at the same instant she did.

She pulled the door open and gazed at the man standing before her. He removed his hat and nodded. "Ma'am."

A large chestnut-colored horse stood by the hitching post behind him. Weathered saddlebags hung on either side of the animal.

The horse had not been secured to the post. Its reins hung down over its head and touched the ground before its front hooves.

"You've forgotten to tie your horse."

"No, ma'am, I haven't. Charles is fine, I assure you."

The man's southern drawl brought a wave of homesickness. It had been a while since she heard words roll off a tongue the way his did.

"Are you sure? He's not tied to the post—aren't you worried he'll run off?"

The man looked over his shoulder toward the animal. Then he turned his attention back on Violet. When he smiled, she involuntarily leaned closer, as if drawn to him by an invisible thread. It made no sense, but her body angled forward.

"Charles is the best stock the other side of the Mississippi can offer. He knows better than to run. He's a horse with character, ma'am. No need to worry." He wore his hair long and now he ran his fingers through it and pushed the brown tendrils away from his face.

He had eyes the color of the Atlantic Ocean. They were deep, dark, vivid blue.

Violet stared. She had seen those eyes before.

"Have we met? A long time ago, maybe?"

His smile grew. "You remember me. I always said that if I lived, I would find the girl who saved my life and thank her. I never make a promise I don't intend to keep."

She gasped.

Her heartbeat quickened. It couldn't be—but it was!

"I'd recognize you anywhere, Miss Bloom. You're still the most beautiful female I've ever had the honor to look upon." He grinned and shifted his weight from one foot to the other. "I would apologize for being so frank, but I can't. I mean every bit of it—you are prettier than you were when you saved my life, and you were a living angel then, ma'am."

"Tate Taylor. Why, as I live and breathe..." Dozens of questions ran through her mind, but she couldn't speak a word. It was enough to stand and stare at the man who she had spent nearly half of her life thinking had perished.

"And I live and breathe, too. Because of you, that is."

His words were tender and touched her heart. Tears

came to her eyes.

Violet threw propriety to the wind and raised her good arm to hug him. Tate dropped his hat, wrapped his arms around her, and pulled her into an embrace that was a genuine Christmas blessing.

Tears fell freely as she held onto the man who she had wondered about for so long. He had made such a profound impression on her that there had not been one day since they met that she did not think about him.

"I believed you were dead."

"I would have been if you hadn't walked by in that hospital."

She hugged him with her one good arm. "I prayed you had lived but I genuinely believed you had died." Violet pulled back so she could see his face. No awkwardness existed between them. Being this close to him felt perfectly fine. "I'm so glad you're alive. This is such a gift, seeing you again. After all these years of wondering, here you are. Who would have imagined such a thing might happen?"

Tate pushed a curl off her cheek with a gentle fingertip. "I have thought about nothing else for years. It has been my life's mission to find you and thank you. Seeing you again, holding you close, staring into your kind eyes…this is a dream come true. Truly, this is everything to me."

"Me, too," Violet whispered.

Chapter 34

Sheriff Earl Hanson stopped by the schoolhouse on Sunday morning to check on the fine horse that stood, unhitched, in front of the building. A man had to be impressed by the animal's training and character. Very few remained in place without an owner in sight. That this one did was something special.

The smoke rising from the chimney on this day also intrigued him. Miss Bloom didn't often keep Sunday hours in the schoolroom. And with the state of her health, he expected she would be resting in that snug home of hers.

He had considered telling her that the Christmas program didn't have to go on if she felt too poorly. Land sakes, the woman had fallen on her head, nearly frozen to death in a snowstorm, been tossed into a root cellar in her undergarments while he and his men tamped down some liquored-up ranch hands, and, to top it off, she had been assaulted on Wylder Street in broad daylight.

Even battered and broken, her spirit seemed indestructible. Still, perhaps they owed it to the new educator to give her a pass on this holiday event. Hard enough to find a decent schoolteacher willing to come all the way out west. It would be a damn shame if they killed this one before her first year was up.

He entered the schoolhouse without bothering to

knock.

The space had been transformed into a winter wonderland.

Colorful garlands were strung along every wall. Decorated pinecones dangled from ribbons.

Two tables were angled in one corner. Folded lengths of fabric rested on their polished tops, ready to be spread out so food would show to its best advantage.

A tree, still undecorated, waited in another corner. Beside it, a wooden riser where the children would perform, he supposed. And on the other side of the Christmas tree, in a place of honor, a high-backed wooden chair. Santa's throne, just waiting for its special visitor.

What caught his attention weren't the decorations or even the festive atmosphere. They were all well and good, but they weren't what most interested the lawman.

There were three people in the room. None had sensed his presence yet, so he freely studied them without their knowledge.

A stranger who moved with a slight stiffness in his shoulder banged a nail into the wall above the ladies' heads in the far corner. The sheriff had enough of his own aches and pains to recognize when a man pushed past a twinge. Probably responsible for the horse waiting outside.

Miss Bloom stood near the man. She pointed with her left hand to a spot high on the wall, to where the nail went into wood.

A third person occupied the room, a trim woman who held a paper garland in her hands. She didn't speak but he didn't need to hear her to see the truth.

The schoolteacher had lied to him. She was in cahoots with the Chinese woman he had been searching for.

"Well, if this isn't a right interestin' holiday scene."

The women whirled to face him with shocked—and, he noted, frightened—expressions on their faces.

The stranger gave the nail a last whack before he turned. When no one replied, he looked from one woman to the other before his friendly smile turned hard.

The sheriff held up a hand and pulled his dark blue bandana away from his coat so the newcomer caught sight of his badge. Then he pushed his jacket back and put his hands on his hips, revealing the two revolvers he wore. No need for any trouble. Not on a Sunday morning, with two women present, in the schoolhouse. He watched as the man's gaze lowered, then rose back to meet his. A quick nod, and the man brought both hands into plain sight.

He turned his attention on the schoolteacher. "Miss Bloom, I believe we have some talking to do, don't you?"

Chapter 35

Telling Sheriff Hanson the truth wasn't as difficult as Violet feared it would be.

She would have preferred Tate not hear about their circumstances, but the sheriff insisted he remain, so she went to the front door, locked it, and dropped the wooden bar down into place. It would not do to have an interruption—or an eavesdropper—while they came clean.

She let Lin tell the tale, mostly. The language barrier required that she assist at some points, but her friend did an excellent job of telling her story on her own.

Violet saw Tate wipe an eye when she showed how her brother had been killed. An understandable soldier's reaction to seeing a shot to the chest, even in pantomime. She wondered how many of Tate's fellow soldiers, friends, or family he had witnessed dying that way. By the hardening of his jawline, she had her answer. There had been some.

The sheriff rose and walked over to the teacher's cupboard. He opened the narrow door, stuck his head inside, and looked at the shelves, extra sweater, and assorted items kept within. Turning back to them, he pointed his thumb to the closet and directed his question toward Lin. "You mean to tell me you spent a whole night and a day inside here?"

A fast nod. "Yes, I lived inside. All night. All day."

He closed the door and walked back over to them. Their chairs were arranged near the stove, but he did not return to his. Instead he stood beside Lin and gazed down at her with unconcealed admiration.

"I have seen a lot of things in my time, ma'am, but I have never seen such a small woman with so much courage. You are a force to be reckoned with. Your wits kept you alive."

Lin looked down at her hands and sighed. "But not brother. They kill him. I could not save." A tear slid down her cheek so Violet reached over and put her arm around her.

The sheriff stepped back, turning to the pile of firewood and choosing a piece. He opened the heavy stove, tossed the log inside, and latched the door. He rubbed his hands together over the stove's flat, cast iron top for a minute.

He returned to his seat. The chair had been intended for a pupil and the man tested its capacity. So far, its legs had held the big man and his slight paunch.

Sheriff Hanson turned to Tate Taylor.

"And you came riding into town to hang garlands? Is that what you'd have me believe?"

Tate didn't take offense at the sheriff's brusque questions.

"No, sir. I learned from Miss Bloom's family—her sister Miss Lily Bloom, to be exact—where to find her out here in the Wyoming territory. I planned to head this way anyhow so I figured I would call on her. The garland came as a surprise."

He grinned at her and, despite the conditions of the moment, she smiled back. Tate's presence lifted her heart better than any gift in any box beneath a tree could have. For so long, she had assumed the worst. But here he sat, with those unforgettable blue eyes, in her schoolroom.

She nearly pinched herself to be sure she wasn't dreaming, but the sheriff would raise an eyebrow over it, so she resisted.

Sheriff Hanson glanced over at Lin. She delicately wiped her eyes on a hanky pulled from her dress pocket. Violet appreciated that the seasoned sheriff gave a distressed woman time to collect herself.

"And how do you know Miss Bloom?" He spared no mercy for Tate. "You must have some strong feelings for the lady, to come all the way to Wylder to see her."

Tate sat back and scrubbed a hand across his chin. "Well, it's quite a story, how we became acquainted."

"I've got all day." The sheriff crossed his arms over his chest and waited.

Fortunately, Tate left out the grisly details. He gave an abbreviated version, one that cast Violet in too high a light in her opinion, but when she demurred, he insisted.

"The lady saved my life. Without her, I'd be resting under a tombstone alongside my own brother, who was killed at Gettysburg. See, I never made it that far. After Miss Bloom saved me from bleeding to death, I spent some time in a hospital before finding my way home."

The sheriff didn't respond so Tate continued.

"I made a promise the day I met this admirable lady. If I lived—and I determined I'd give it my best to do so—I would find her and thank her someday. Today, it seems, is that day. After all these years, I'm here to thank Miss Bloom for saving my life."

"Really, I didn't do anything special. I happened to be in the right spot at the right time." Her face warmed, and she knew the heat didn't come from the woodstove.

Sheriff Hanson stroked his beard as he met her gaze. "It sounds like you've been saving lives for a while now, doesn't it?" He looked to Lin. "I have a few more questions to ask, if you're up to it."

She gave a fast chin dip. "Yes."

"So, you're telling me that you're the last survivor of an ancient family line and that the men who are trying to kill you will gain the family treasure if you die. Is that right?"

She and Lin both nodded.

"I've been tracking these Chinese killers for a while. Don't look so flabbergasted—your brother isn't the first person they've killed. He seems to be the only one they've murdered with intent. The others have been average guys, people who got in their way."

Violet shot him a questioning look, one she generally reserved for when she suspected a pupil of withholding information from her.

"So, you knew there were Chinese murderers on the loose when you stopped me to ask if I knew of a Chinese woman who suddenly appeared in town? You were aware of a problem when you asked me those questions, weren't you?"

He didn't try to hide the truth. A slow drop of his chin to his chest, then back up. "I sure did. You don't think I've been sheriff this long without understanding how to track the lawless, do you? Of course I knew—and I had a feeling you were hiding something that morning, but I just couldn't put my finger on it."

"But you didn't tell me there are murderers on the loose. Why not?"

He shook his head as the edges of his lips pulled up. The white beard couldn't hide his amusement. "Have you forgotten where you are? Ma'am, there are murderers, scoundrels of all kinds, and unruly fools lurking around every corner out here in the west. I don't have time to warn every citizen about every villain—there aren't enough hours in the day."

"I appreciate that. So now that you know Lin's story, you see she didn't kill her brother, don't you? And you must see that she needs protection—her life depends on it. You must catch those Chinese bad men so she can live in peace."

Tate cleared his throat. "That's a tall order. I'm quite sure the sheriff here has a lot going on, and finding murderers isn't as easy as all that."

"I'm not trying to be unreasonable, but Lin has no one else but us. She has no people—the only one she has is me, and the folks in town who will become her family if she agrees to remain in Wylder. That is, if we can keep her alive."

Sheriff Hanson looked at Lin. "One last question for you, Miss Sun. Rumor has it that the Chinese men are after a large, valuable black pearl. Do you know anything about that?"

Lin giggled, surprising them all. Violet had never asked her about the pearl. It had actually slipped her mind with everything else that had happened.

Placing a hand on her chest, the Chinese woman said, "My people have legend. Last princess is precious like black pearl. I am the pearl." She covered her mouth with her hand and giggled again. Sharing her story had been good medicine. Lin's shoulders were not held as rigidly high as they had been, and she looked less frightened.

"We still need to find those men," Violet insisted.

"You're right." The sheriff nodded thoughtfully. "But how? We need to lure them into a trap and the only one I can think to set is right here, at the Christmas party on Tuesday. Unfortunately, Miss Sun would have to be the bait for that trap."

They all glanced at each other as they considered their options.

Tate's brow furrowed and his navy eyes blazed.

Lin's smile fell away.

Violet looked at the sheriff. "If you consent to be our Santa Claus, you'll be in the midst of the trap. I'd be more comfortable with you close by to protect Lin. I don't want them to hurt her, so please, say you'll do it."

Sheriff Hanson studied his boot tips. Then he met her gaze and gave a wise nod. "Do you have a red suit, or do I have to find one of my own?" Patting his belly, he winked. "I already come with padding."

Chapter 36

Violet marked items off her mental checklist.

The schoolhouse waited for the Christmas party, as decorated as a festive package ready to be unwrapped.

Tate had secured a room at Culpepper's Boarding House. He and the sheriff planned to grab dinner and a drink later at the Five Star Saloon before turning in for the night. They had hit it off, which pleased Violet very much.

She still could hardly believe that Tate had survived the war, but it was true. And that he resided in Wylder, even temporarily, made it even better.

Now that their secrets were with the sheriff, Lin might remain safe. With any luck, the Christmas party would entice the murderers so the lawmen could grab them. And then she would be able to live her life without fear.

After a quiet midday meal, Violet could have taken a nap but there were still some details to be attended to before the holiday.

Lin had other ideas. "You sit. Time to rest now." She had no shyness about using her growing English vocabulary.

"I will, I promise. But first I need to ask you for a favor." She motioned for Lin to accompany her into her bedroom.

The largest piece of furniture in the house, a pine

wardrobe, stood in one corner. Her modest collection of clothing didn't begin to fill it but having extra storage space would prove beneficial as she accumulated possessions. It made her happy to have somewhere other than wall hooks to hang her clothes. So many homes didn't have luxuries like this.

Frankly, it surprised her that a single man would build a piece of furniture like the wardrobe, but she had given up trying to figure out what motivated a man she had never met. Jasper Abraham would remain as much a mystery to her as the massive piece of furniture he had built for the home they would never share.

She opened the wardrobe door. Two of the dresses hanging inside were better suited to Charleston parties than the Wylder schoolroom. Plus, while they were lovely, they were both a bit snug now that she had finally put a few womanly curves onto her slender form.

They would look beautiful on Lin, though.

Almost the color of a fine port wine, the maroon dress had a matching shawl. The other, a sapphire blue, featured a fitted bodice. Looking at it reminded her of Tate Taylor's eyes, but she shook the thought out of her mind as she placed the dresses on the bed.

"I know they aren't royal or fit for a princess, but I believe you will make either look stunning. You need a dress for the Christmas party. I think we can make one of these over to fit you if you would like."

Lin ran a slow hand over the full skirts of first the maroon dress, then the blue. She fingered the fabric and sighed. "So beautiful."

Violet felt it right to add, "If you prefer, we can go to Lowery's Dress Shop tomorrow to see if there is anything there that you might like better."

The woman who already felt like a sister shook her head before she even finished speaking. So, apparently Lin's comprehension skills were improving, too!

"No—no dress shop. Please, I like these. Very much."

Lin reached out and gave her a gentle hug. She carefully avoided the bandaged arm, but the unexpected gesture gave Violet's mood an enormous boost. She had been hiding it but being away from Charleston for Christmas had been making her exceedingly homesick. Lin's loving act came at precisely the right moment.

"You may have them both. Which one would you like to wear Tuesday evening? We should see what alterations it needs, although I'm not sure I will be much help with that." She held up the bandaged arm. Lin had been doing almost everything around the house. She helped Violet dress and undress, as well. "Do you sew, Lin? Is that a skill women learn in China?"

Lin considered the question for a moment before she grinned. Then, looking less like a princess and more like a mischievous child, she unbuttoned the shirtwaist Violet had given her to wear.

Lin pulled it open, revealing the white cotton undershirt Violet had purchased at the mercantile. No longer plain and unadorned, intricate black stitching turned the front into a wonderland. Lin had created a garden scene complete with a building, winding river, and flowers. Chinese characters danced up one side of the garment and lacy curlicues adorned the neckline.

Violet stared at the stunning needlework, overwhelmed by the beauty. Lin had brought her home to life.

"That is China, isn't it?"

Lin buttoned the shirt. "Yes, is my home."

"It is delightful, Lin. But tell me, where did you find the thread? I have a sewing basket with many colors of thread that you are welcome to use. Why did you choose black—is it symbolic in some way?"

She waited while Lin formulated her reply.

"No—no symbolic. I use thread from clothing I wore. Man's clothing? I had needle in my bag."

Lin had taken thread from the men's garments she had worn to elude capture and death and had used it to create something beautiful.

"I fix this one?" Lin held the blue up to her body and did a little swaying motion. The skirt swished around her ankles, covering her feet, and showing that they would need to enlarge the hem.

"Princess, we will fix that one for you to wear on Tuesday."

At her use of the title, Lin covered her face with the dress and dissolved into a fit of giggles. Violet joined her and for the first time all week, she felt that things were going to turn out well for both of them.

Chapter 37

As the afternoon shadows grew long, they heard heavy footsteps on the front porch. Then, a thud.

Lin dropped her sewing onto the settee and Violet put her book on the table beside the chair. They had discussed this possibility earlier.

They hurried to the kitchen. Lin rushed into the pantry closet and settled in as silently as a church mouse. Violet patted the left-hand pocket of her skirt, the weight of the derringer reassuring as she went to answer the door.

She peeked out the side window but didn't see anyone. She waited, in case someone hid on the other side of the small porch. No one showed themselves so she put her hand on the latch, took a deep breath, and opened the door a crack.

No one jumped out at her so she opened it a few more inches.

She looked down.

In a metal pot on the wooden flooring sat the cutest little pine tree. A length of burlap covered its base and a red-and-green plaid bow wrapped around the top branch.

Violet leaned down and grasped the metal handle on the pot with her good hand. She dragged it across the porch floor, over the threshold, and into the front room. Ever mindful of their circumstances, she went and locked the door before she ran to the kitchen to unlatch the pantry closet.

Violet reached out and took Lin's hand. She tugged her to the front room so they could share the Christmas gift.

"Look! Someone left us a Christmas tree—isn't it beautiful?"

Lin still struggled to comprehend the holiday and its traditions. They had discussed it at length, but Violet wasn't sure her friend completely understood the nature of the observance. She knew it involved a baby and gifts, and that seemed to make sense to her. But Santa, singing, and trees were still troublesome spots. Violet hadn't mentioned the naughty and nice list or coal and stockings—and she had certainly not broached the idea that Santa visited homes while children slept.

"It is tree. Like tree at schoolhouse?"

"Yes, that's right. It is like the one at the schoolhouse, but much smaller. This one is for us." She touched the plaid bow and felt her heart flutter. She hadn't realized how much she missed a decorated house until this very instant.

"Who bring tree here?"

She turned to face the other woman. "Lin, your English is getting so much better. Really, you must be sleeping with that reader I brought home. I wish my pupils were this eager to learn."

Lin blushed. "I enjoy learning." She pointed to the tree. "Tree?"

"I have no idea. There doesn't seem to be a note attached anywhere. I suppose it could have come from any of my pupils." She ran through the list of families in her mind but found no obvious choice. Most of her pupils were from families that were scrabbling to make a living. No one could afford any extras, not really.

But if it grew free somewhere it made an ideal surprise.

Yes, that must be it.

"I think someone dug it up for us. It came from their property, I'm sure of it." A finger of doubt tickled the back of her neck, but she swatted it away. "What else could it be? No one would spend money on a Christmas tree for us, so it must be from a homestead. Yes, it has to be one of my frontier families."

"We decorate? Like at schoolhouse?" Lin tilted her head with a hopeful smile on her face. "Make pretty?"

Chapter 38

An hour later the tree sparkled. It didn't take much to dress it up, and they took great pleasure in working holiday magic on the fragrant branches.

Lin constructed a straw birds' nest with a cotton-and-feather bird for one branch. They strung cranberries for a garland that they would eat after the holiday. Bits of spare ribbon were tied into bows on some branches. Two glass icicles sent firelight dancing on the walls and ceiling. When Violet brought out a teeny-tiny candle to place on the sturdiest branch, Lin clapped her hands.

"We shall wait until Christmas Day to light this. I would say we would do so before then but I only have the one candle that size so we shall have to cultivate anticipation for the tree lighting."

Lin brought her eyebrows together and gave her a questioning look.

"You're right, that is a mouthful. I'm sorry. How about we look forward to lighting the candle? Is that better?"

"Much better. Thank you."

They returned to their individual Sunday afternoon pursuits.

Violet picked up her book. She couldn't find it in her heart to read the one from Thomas, so she fell into a Louisa May Alcott volume.

Lin went back to her sewing.

The front door became the victim of a new wave of knocking. This time, a few stuttering raps followed by silence. Then two more.

"Good heavens. Wylder on a Sunday is almost too busy for my liking." Violet rose, patted her skirt pocket more from habit than anything else at this point, and accompanied Lin to the kitchen pantry cupboard. "I'm sorry—I shall dispense with whoever that is as quickly as possible."

She latched the pantry door and headed toward the front door—again.

And again, she checked through the small window beside the door to see who knocked.

When the man on the porch turned to gaze at her through the window, Violet nearly fainted dead away.

Jasper Abraham, the man she had come to Wylder to wed, stood outside. He had, as everyone knew, died the week before Violet's arrival.

Apparently, no one had informed the man that he had been deceased for eight long months because he smiled and gave a nonchalant wave before pointing to the door and mouthing the words, "Open the door."

Violet let the curtain fall back into place over the glass.

Jasper Abraham.

He had sent a likeness of himself when they were corresponding. The man who stood on the other side of the door looked identical to the man whose photograph she'd carried across thousands of miles. It remained tucked inside her journal because she hadn't had the heart to throw it away.

Oh, damn! What if he wants to marry me?

Panic turned her mind to stone.

She had no idea how long she stood there like Lot's wife, turned immobile as punishment for her evil ways.

He knocked again and she jumped.

If he had a key, he might decide to use it. Right now, she didn't know much, but she knew she didn't want him inside the house.

She couldn't keep Lin locked in a pantry cupboard forever. Trapping the poor woman indefinitely wouldn't do.

Only one course of action presented itself.

She put her mouth close to the door and called, "I'll be right out."

Then she returned to the kitchen and released her friend from her hiding spot. There was no time to explain, so she didn't try. She merely told Lin that an acquaintance arrived unexpectedly, and she would meet with him on the porch.

Violet took her heaviest shawl from the hook and wrapped it around her shoulders. She patted her skirt pocket. Then she opened the front door and slipped outside.

Chapter 39

In the deepening gloom, Violet stared at the man responsible for her coming to Wylder. Fear constricted her throat. Her skirts covered her shaking knees, and she buried her trembling hands in the folds of the shawl.

Determined to not be the first to speak, she waited. Let him identify himself and explain why she had arrived to find him supposedly dead when it was apparent that he remained among the living.

If he could be stubborn enough to stay away for all this time, she could certainly be obstinate enough to stare him down.

He put his hat on the table beside the door and held his hands out in a show of good faith. The gesture that he meant no harm died when he raised his hands and his jacket hiked up. She got a look at the pistols hanging from the worn gun belt slung low across his hips. His intentions were yet to be seen. The fact showed that he came prepared to do some damage.

The derringer in her pocket would give her one chance to defend herself if it came to that.

She hoped it wouldn't be necessary, but shooting him if he threatened her would not disturb her at all.

"Miss Bloom." He tipped his head and gave her a cautious smile. "It is a pleasure to finally make your acquaintance."

She bit her tongue, determined to let him explain on his own. She would not pepper him with questions that would make his account less taxing. He owed her the truth, and she planned to get it.

"Mister Abraham."

"I saw you take a look at my sidearms. You've no need to be afeared."

"Oh, I assure you, I'm not afraid of you."

"I don't blame you for having your dander up. I deserve all the wrath I'm sure you plan to hurl at me." He scratched at a spot near his ear before he pulled at the faded bandana tied around his neck. "I hope you give me the chance to defend myself first. Then, renounce me as the lowliest skunk to ever live. I have already chastised myself many times and I know I should be dragged behind a mule."

A wooden bench sat on the porch in full view of the small window beside the door, so she settled herself there.

She did not invite him to sit.

"I am listening. This is the first time I have given audience to a dead man."

He shuddered and twisted his hands together. "I deserve that. But please, allow me to explain."

Violet held her shawl with her right hand and put the left into her pocket. "Go on."

He leaned a hip against the front door. "I will make this as uncomplicated as possible. When we began our correspondence, I told you I needed a bride. Those words were true...to an extent."

"To an extent? What does that mean?"

He placed his hands together in supplication. "I beg you, please let me tell you what I need to say, in my way. When I am done, I will answer your questions. I give you my word."

"Your word? It seems a tad late for that."

His hands came together again.

She pursed her lips and willed herself to remain silent.

"I may as well say the worst part first: I am married."

Violet kept her lips closed and waited for him to continue.

"When I advertised for a mail-order bride I had been informed, in no uncertain terms, that I would soon be unmarried. My wife set to tellin' me how unhappy our marriage made her. She planned to divorce me on grounds of moral corruption and abandonment." He yanked at the bandana again. When he swallowed, his Adam's apple slid high and low on his skinny neck. "She had a whole lot of other ugly lies to tell, too. Her words and actions were so discombobulating that I immediately placed that advert for a bride. You see, some of us are not equipped to be on our own."

He paused, as if waiting for her to question him, but she did not. No, she had agreed to hear him out and intended to do just that.

The man's hair was an unusual shade of sandy brown. Now he ran a hand through it and pushed it back off his temples.

"While we were corresponding, I believed Elizabeth—that's my wife—was settin' to divorce me. She even sent me a legal letter, although I don't know what it said because I put it in the kitchen stove and burned the damn thing. Oh, excuse me, Miss Bloom. I forget myself."

Violet had heard enough. Her gut churned and a vein beat in her temple. It might feel satisfying to shoot him in a nonessential spot. Let him get a taste of how it smarted to be hurt.

"You are a married man who asked an unmarried schoolteacher to travel clear across the civilized world with an offer of marriage, and you're concerned about swearing? You are a man with an exceedingly small conscience."

He bowed his head for a long moment before meeting her gaze. "I deserve that. I did not know Beth had reconsidered when I made my offer to you. She dropped every untrue charge against me...and she pleaded for a second chance." He shrugged, and his shirt slipped from the waistband of his roomy denim jeans. Beneath his jacket, he hardly had any meat on his bones. "What could I do? I went to her and we have remained married. You see, I didn't deliberately mislead you. We got caught in a regrettable chain of events."

"A chain that left me alone in a place I had never been to."

He nodded. "Yes. Lamentably, that is so."

"But the townsfolk buried a dead man in the bone yard across the tracks. Who is that?"

His face crumpled in on itself. "My twin brother had consumption. We were so close. He is buried in the cemetery. I visited his grave a short time ago."

Violet considered all that he had confessed. He hadn't intentionally misled her. She saw how it came about, and almost felt sorry for the man.

"Why are you here now?"

He heaved a huge sigh. "I have always had a soft

spot in my heart for this holiday. Christmas is the season of forgiveness. I admit, I am having a rough time living with what I've done. I'm here to come clean, and to implore you to forgive me."

Jasper wasn't the only one who had entered into their association falsely.

Time to confess.

"I did not want to marry you, Mister Abraham." She swallowed before she forced the next words out. "You see, I merely wanted to get away from Charleston, and I would have done anything to do so."

Jasper took a step back. He placed his palms flat on his coat above his chest and shook his head. "Including marry me?"

She met his gaze and admitted the truth. "I'm sorry, but yes. I would have done anything to get clear of Charleston, including marrying a man I didn't love."

When he came closer, she scooted over on the bench. Her heart had softened, and since the bench provided ample room for them to sit comfortably, she made the concession. He smiled his thanks and sat down.

"But why? You are a beautiful woman. You didn't need to answer any mail-order advert—I know that you must have had your pick of men to marry. Why do it? I don't understand."

Now that she decided to tell it, the truth came with ease.

"I had suitors in Charleston. But I could not see a life in that city, not after having lived through the war there and witnessing all the death and destruction. It felt as if I were paying for something I never did—I had been sentenced for a crime someone else had committed. Charleston is not the same as before the war. And I couldn't live through a lifetime in that sad city."

"So, you answered my advertisement?"

"I thought I could come here and find some joy in a town that has not been marked by sadness or soaked in blood. I wanted a fresh start, a place that offered opportunities for the future. Somewhere not stuck in the past."

It hit her that in some respects she still held on to that past, trying to make others suffer for blood that had been spilled long ago.

"That makes perfect sense, Miss Bloom."

Thomas's face came to mind. His gentle touch and kind words, too.

"Miss Bloom?"

"I'm sorry—I guess I got stuck in the past."

He reached over and patted her hand. No one witnessed the inappropriate gesture, and it did not insult her one bit. In every practical sense, Jasper belonged to the realm of the dead. How could a dead man behave improperly?

"We all have a past." He threaded his fingers together and placed them on one thigh. "Some, like this feller here, get caught up holding on to what we should walk away from. We miss out on what might have been the best thing to happen to us."

Violet turned to face him. They stared into each other's eyes for a long while, as they had at the beginning of this conversation. Much had changed in a short amount of time.

Acceptance replaced anger.

Clarity chased away confusion.

And where there had been irrational attachment to history, hope of letting go had been born.

Violet had never hugged a dead man but before Jasper Abraham left to return to his wife, she hugged him good and hard.

Chapter 40

Monday morning came with red skies.

Shakespeare came to mind, particularly "Venus and Adonis" where he lamented that the red skies of morning heralded wrecks to seamen and sorrows to shepherds.

Well, being neither seamen nor shepherd, she did not fret over the poet's discourse. Instead, she stood on her porch and stared, in awe of the streaks of crimson and rose that swept above Wylder. They looked like ribbons wrapping the town up like one giant Christmas gift.

To those who ventured into the territory, the rugged spot filled with quirky characters provided a new beginning. Life was harsh on the frontier but well worth any difficulties one encountered.

She had arrived in town on the wings of deceit, false promises, and desperation. Certainly, she wasn't the only one who came here under less-than-honorable circumstances, but she had done her best to do better, and to do right by the place and people who had taken her in.

Finding a home here was a meaningful gift she intended to keep, always.

It might take some doing but she planned on unraveling any remaining bits of false thinking that had traveled with her from South Carolina. She might be a schoolteacher, but she had learned a few lessons of her own since her arrival.

The old ways must remain in the past if she were to have any chance at happiness. Time to leave the horror behind because if she harbored hatred in her heart, the difficult memories she attempted to outrun would doggedly follow her every step. The lesson had been a long time coming.

Red skies. Bright wrappings. New beginnings.

Well, nothing can change as long as I stand here staring out at the world.

Violet walked the short distance to the schoolhouse, glad no snow had fallen overnight. Last Monday's tumble into her personal snowy nightmare still lived fresh in her mind and she did not want a repeat of that madness anytime soon.

She paused at the stone wishing well in front of the schoolhouse. Running a hand across the cold surface, she considered what her wish might be. In the past she felt silly contemplating the subject. She thought wishes and wells were fine for children but ridiculous for adults.

Now, she did not feel ridiculous.

With one last glance at the pink ribbons in the sky, she faced the sad truth. Her chance to fulfill her deepest wish had come to her, and she had pushed it away. Opportunities like that did not happen more than once in a lifetime.

Lamenting what is lost served no purpose so she turned and walked toward the schoolhouse door. A lot to do before Christmas Eve meant she didn't have time to waste.

If she were still in Charleston, Mother would say

that occupied minds and working hands kept one safe from melancholy. Taking her mother's long-distance advice to heart, Violet straightened her shoulders and busied herself preparing for the day ahead.

She managed to get the fire in the belly stove up to a steady roar and the space began to warm. It would be midday before the schoolroom felt truly cozy but at least the children wouldn't shake in their seats during morning lessons.

The day's lessons would be rudimentary. She couldn't expect her pupils to concentrate fully on book learning with Christmas looming. There would be time for individualized reading, a drawing lesson, and then she would read some poetry to them which they would discuss.

Discussions about readings brought some of her favorite moments with her pupils. Their talks were lively because she encouraged everyone to participate. Many children lived in homes where children were seen and not heard. So, at school she made sure they were all heard.

The biggest challenge of the morning came with putting her daily quote up on the chalkboard. She wrote with her right hand which was, unfortunately, attached to the broken arm and far from being healed.

She tried writing with the left, but that penmanship was of such poor quality that even her most advanced pupils would not decipher it.

When she heard the front door open and the first footsteps of the morning hit the scuffed wooden floorboards, she still struggled at the chalkboard.

She turned to see who arrived so early on this Monday morning.

Thomas and Alexia Harvey stood by the entrance. They wore uncertain smiles.

Violet went to greet her new pupil.

"Alexia, I am so glad to see you are joining us. Welcome to the Wylder School where we learn all the basics and much, much more."

A couple of nights of rest, some substantial meals, and warm baths had proved beneficial. Thomas's daughter looked as shiny as a brand-new silver dollar.

"Thank you, Miss Bloom." She paused and glanced up at her father. He gave her a barely discernible nod, so she returned her gaze to her new teacher and added, "I am sorry for my behavior when we last met. I was wrong, and I disrespected you, my father, my aunt, and all of Wylder with my words. I hope you will forgive me. I promise to never be that hateful again, ma'am."

Violet had heard many apologies in her time but none as sincere as this one. She fought the urge to gather the girl into her arms. The child might be put off by such a display. After all, she did not have a mother to lavish attention on her and might not be familiar with such energetic care.

"Apology accepted." She looked over at the man whose gaze revealed nothing of his own feelings. Then she put a hand on the girl's shoulder and gave her a reassuring squeeze. "We all do things we regret. And we all hope to find mercy from those we have wronged. It is part of life and it is a lesson for us. Do you know what that lesson is?"

Alexia shook her head. "No, ma'am."

"The life lesson is that we should realize when we are wrongly thinking and search for forgiveness—and perhaps a second chance to behave properly. That is what we are meant to learn. I shall share a secret with you: Adults still work to learn that. It does not end when one is grown, I'm afraid."

"Yes, ma'am. I will remember that."

"Why don't you take your coat off? Hang it on one of the hooks over there on the wall. And do you see that last seat in the back row? I've assigned that one to you, so you may put your things on that bench."

"Thank you, ma'am."

The girl went to hang her coat.

Violet met Thomas's gaze.

They met a week ago, but it felt as if she had known him for a lifetime.

It crossed her mind to make her own apology to the man, and hope he forgave as easily as she did. But the sound of horse hooves and carriage wheels met their ears.

This was not the time for them to speak.

He looked over at the chalkboard and wrinkled his brow. "I don't wish to appear impolite, but whatever is that supposed to mean?"

Violet held up her right arm. Lin had wrapped it this morning in a dark blue length of worsted to match the skirt she wore.

"That makes sense. You can't write with an arm trussed up that way." He put a hand out, palm up. She still held the chalk between her fingers, but she passed it over to him. "What are you trying to write?"

They went to the front of the room as the door opened and a wave of excited, chattering pupils entered. The children knew to put their outdoor clothing on hooks and take their seats.

He used the rag by the board to wipe away her

scrawl. "Well? What shall I write for your schoolroom to ruminate on today?"

"I would appreciate it if you would write a line from Mister Dickens's *A Christmas Carol*. It goes like this: 'There is nothing in the world so irresistibly contagious as laughter and good humor.'"

When he finished writing he turned to her and winked. "I must admit, I heartily agree with Mister Dickens. Good day, Miss Bloom."

Chapter 41

The Wylder School did not open its doors to students on Tuesday.

First thing in the morning, while many still slept in their beds, Violet and Lin, as well as Tate and Sheriff Hanson, readied the schoolroom for the community get-together. It had been cleaned, decorated, and gussied up to its greatest good. The fire was laid and ready, candles waited to be kindled, and Santa's throne had been festooned with greens wrapped around a swatch of red velvet.

Nothing remained to be done. Stockings were hung, and peace had come to the little schoolhouse.

That could not be said for the entire town.

By the time they finished, Wylder bustled. The town looked as busy as Violet imagined the rooms inside the Social Club did after ranch hands received their monthly pay. There were people everywhere.

Wagons from homesteads trundled down Wylder Street. Pine boughs hung from buckboards and sacks nestled near feet, warming toes and staying safe from prying eyes. Children waved from the backs of wagons, calling to schoolmates about the party, home preparations, or Santa.

Merchants hung wreaths and garlands from front doors and hitching posts. The scent of pine competed with the usual smells of horse manure and rarely washed bodies.

Passersby nodded and smiled and were friendlier than usual. The festive atmosphere wrapped the town in benevolence that could almost be tasted on the tongue.

Violet and Lin walked arm in arm down Wylder Street.

Lin had been reluctant to go out but if they were to catch the Chinese villains, they must bait the trap and let them see the princess alive and well. They emerged from the schoolhouse, and with Tate lagging inconspicuously behind to give them protection, felt almost safe.

Neither could relax until the men who had killed Lin's brother were brought to justice. There would probably be a necktie social for the pair, and then their threat would be forever eliminated. It couldn't happen soon enough.

Violet didn't abide unnecessary killing, but she didn't feel badly when those who murdered got a taste of their own medicine.

She had a short list of stops to make before they went home to dress for the party. Lin wanted to go to the mercantile, so they went there first.

The sight of the mercantile, crowded as a church on Easter Sunday morning, stopped them just inside the door. There were so many in the building that the aisles were jammed.

With a shake of her head, Violet reminded herself that thriving businesses were beneficial to everyone in town—even if that meant she might have to wait for her turn at the counter or elbow her way past browsers.

"We go fast?" Lin did not like crowds. They had discussed her childhood as a princess in China and she indicated that she felt shy in public during large gatherings, like parades.

This must seem like a nightmare to her.

"Yes, we will get what we need and leave."

"I go…" Lin pointed to the far side of the shop. She waved her hand between them. "You do not come, please?"

"Ah, of course. But please, don't leave the mercantile without me."

"No leave—I will wait here when done."

Violet hated to let her go, but at Christmas everyone had secrets to tend, so she nodded. Then she met Tate's gaze and tipped her head toward Lin's retreating figure. When he trailed her, she released the breath she'd held. Tate would keep Lin safe.

She headed to the sweets counter. Peppermints for the children were already in the stockings hanging in the schoolroom but she discovered that Lin also had a fondness for peppermint. While they stuffed the stockings together, she noticed how many times her friend inhaled the aroma. When asked about it, Lin admitted that her maternal grandmother had kept a jar of mints on her bedside table, and that she encouraged her grandchildren to take a mint whenever they visited.

Lin had many hard, sad memories. Violet meant to nurture the few joyful ones that traveled all the way from China to find a home in Wylder. She had a beautiful cut-glass jar that she had brought from South Carolina. She planned to fill it with mints and place it beneath their Christmas tree for Lin.

She paid for the mints, picked up her package, and turned to leave.

Thomas Harvey stood near the counter. He grinned

at her when she met his gaze.

He removed his hat, ran a hand through his hair to push it back off his face, and waited for her to move away from the small crowd who had gathered to either pay Finn Wylder or pepper him with requests. When she came close, he pointed and said, "I see you have a sweet tooth."

She tucked the package into her bag. "Why, Mister Harvey, what woman doesn't?"

Teasing came naturally between them, the same way conversations and dining together had. He seemed as delighted to see her as she was to see him.

"I take it you have a fondness for mints. I would have predicted you were more a chocolate kind of woman, to be honest."

"Oh, really? Whatever gave you that impression?"

He ran a hand across his chin, as if deep in thought. "Well, from what I've seen, you are a woman of refinement."

"Mints are refined."

"Yes, of course they are, but you are also a woman who has varied interests. Poetry, Mister Dickens, leaping like a frog, sharing wise advice with sorrowful, motherless young women…" He paused, having gone from teasing into more serious territory. Slapping his hat against his thigh, he looked down for a moment before raising his handsome face to catch her gaze again. "A woman who has so many interests and is unique in so many ways? Why, I would think she would appreciate some fine chocolates. You know the ones with caramel, chocolate, vanilla cream, or even nut centers? Those seem more to your liking, but I could be wrong. I've been wrong about a lot of things this past year. This past week, even."

The other shoppers and the bustle of the mercantile fell away. Violet felt insulated and secure, as if they were in a world within the outside world. She neither heard nor saw the others. And she did not care what they were doing—or even what they thought.

All that mattered, in that moment, was Thomas Harvey, and the way his deep, dark eyes invited her to fall into them.

There were so many things she wanted to say to him. Mostly, she wanted to apologize for her bad behavior, but this wasn't the time or place.

"You're not wrong. Chocolates with assorted centers are my favorite. And, indeed, you're not the only one who can be wrong." She swallowed, trying not to cry and embarrass herself. "I've been incorrect about a lot of things, for a long time, it seems. But beliefs can change—I learned that very recently and I plan to work on that part of my thinking."

They stood near the small hand tools, one of the least-crowded spots in the store. Mallets, hand planes, pliers, and saws were not finding their places in Santa's sack this year.

He took a step closer and the aroma of tobacco and wood smoke that came from his jacket went up into her head—and straight to her heart. Whatever happened between them, she would forever connect those scents with this man.

"We need to talk in private. There are things I need to say to you, things I need you to hear." He paused, then lowered his voice even further. "There are things that I need to explain to you, and afterward, if you don't want anything to do with me, I will abide by that. But please, we need to talk."

Nearly identical to the sentiment that had come from Jasper Abraham such a short time ago. *"Christmas is the season of forgiveness."*

Jasper's sentiment hit her like a cannonball. If she could forgive him, she could forgive anyone—including Thomas.

"I agree. We do need to talk." Gertie swung around the far side of the aisle and headed their way. "But not here." She took a step back and put a smile on her face. "Yes, Mister Harvey, your Alexia is quite the pupil. I am glad to have her in the schoolroom."

"Miss Bloom, that is so kind of you. Alexia came home yesterday full of life, so happy to be in the Wylder School and tickled to make some new friends. In particular, she mentioned a girl named Brenda."

"Oh, yes. Brenda Milligan—I sat Alexia right beside her, hoping they would get on well. It's nice to hear they have."

She smiled when Gertie stopped to chat but before she could say anything a commotion broke out on the far side of the mercantile. Boxes thudded to the floor and a string of expletives filled the air.

Violet looked over for Lin, but she did not see her anywhere.

Chapter 42

Finn Wylder's gentle brown eyes bulged, his cheeks showed red, and he had to raise his voice to be heard but he finally gained control of the scene. Two women fighting over the last red chemise did not bring a festive air to his mercantile. Both intended to give their menfolk a bit of a holiday surprise, but they got the surprise when the lacy fabric tore in two. The proprietor insisted each pay a share for the ruined merchandise.

The crowd from the mercantile emptied into the street after the ruckus had been quelled.

"That scared me when I couldn't see you. I worried that something happened to you, Lin." Violet put her good arm through her companion's as they made their way through the crowds. She steered them toward the opposite side of the street where it wasn't quite so busy.

"I am…fine. Yes, fine. I wait by door, like we agree." The wise Chinese woman glanced over her shoulder and nodded to the man behind them. "Mister Tate watch me all time we are in store. No worry."

Thank goodness for Tate's vigilant eye. She wasn't nearly as jumpy as she would have been had he not been observing them.

"I'd like to go in there for a minute." She pointed to Liu Wei's gemstone shop. A wisp of smoke rose from the small building's chimney.

197

Liu Wei opened the door with a charming smile and welcoming nod. Today the slender man wore loose black pants, black shirt, and an intricately embroidered brown vest. The vest's deep brown color matched his eyes perfectly. A pattern woven into the fabric made it look like the scales of a dragon.

"So glad to see you looking so well, Miss Bloom. A healthy pink glow has returned to your cheeks and you seem much improved."

She introduced Sun Lin to Mister Liu. They each placed their palms together and inclined their heads. It looked very regal and proper—and although they had decided not to share Lin's identity, the man seemed to recognize royalty.

The pair chatted in Chinese for a few short minutes. Animated and lyrical, the conversation brought smiles to both faces. It saddened Violet to hear it end.

When she had taught Lin enough English to get by, she intended to request Chinese lessons. She wanted to learn some words and phrases. There might be Chinese pupils in the schoolroom one day, so she ought to know how to converse with them.

Time enough for that chat at a later moment. It was Christmas Eve, and time moved swiftly.

Violet held her breath, hoping for a positive reply when she asked, "Do you have my package ready, Mister Liu?"

He tipped his chin as he reached behind the counter. Handing her a small black velvet box, he said, "I do have it. And I hope it brings the wearer much good luck."

She had paid for the item when she asked him to

make it, so she tucked it into her bag. "Thank you very much. I trust we will see you later today, at the schoolhouse. You know the holiday festivities will be something special this year, don't you?"

He glanced at Lin, who had been watching him from beneath her long, black eyelashes.

"I would not miss it for anything." He smiled so brightly at Lin that he made the sun seem dull by comparison. "It will be, I am sure, the event of the year."

Chapter 43

They exchanged some Christmas gifts early because Violet wanted Lin to be able to wear her gift to the party.

Violet watched Lin open the black velvet box.

Lin's eyes filled with tears when she saw the necklace and for an instant Violet wanted to grab it back. But the awestruck Chinese woman lifted the gift from the box and let it hang from her fingertip.

A polished black pearl dangled from a delicate gold chain.

Lin looked up and whispered, "The black pearl."

"I know nothing can ever be as beautiful as you are and there's no way to restore your cherished family, but I want you to know that you are loved and welcome here. And while I can't replace what's been taken from your life, I respect it—and I respect you. I hope you like it, Lin."

"I have lost much. But I have also gained much." She ran a loving fingertip over the pearl as her lips pulled up at the corners. "I had a home and family. But I still have that. You are family now. Thank you very much, my Violet."

It was the longest speech the woman had given. Violet's eyes were awash with unshed tears. She smiled through the emotion, put her hand out, and took the necklace. Lin held up her cascade of shining black curls and waited for the chain to be clasped around her neck.

Lin turned, put a hand to the pearl, and then wrapped her arms around Violet. "Thank you."

"You're very welcome. Merry Christmas, Lin. It looks lovely with that blue dress."

When the dress had been Violet's it did not have pockets, but Lin's talent as a seamstress had improved the garment. She had added pockets, and now she pulled a tightly folded bundle from one hidden in the side seam.

"Merry Christmas, Violet."

The package was paper, tied with a thin red ribbon fashioned into a bow. She didn't want to untie the gorgeous bow, but Lin urged her forward, waving her hands to the small square bundle and pantomiming pulling at the ends of the ribbons.

"But it's too pretty to unwrap."

"No, no—must unwrap. Pretty is inside, too."

Violet tugged on the ribbon ends and watched the eight loops on the elaborate bow unfold one by one. When they untied, the ribbons hung out of a flat bundle of delicately folded paper. Lin urged her to unfold the packet.

The paper opened to create a three-dimensional landscape. There were trees, flowers, a long-billed goose, and a heart in the little scene. That Lin had cut and folded this artwork was astounding but the heart held an even greater surprise.

Nestled in the center of the cut-paper treasure, right in the middle of the heart, lay a black pearl. It was tiny but flawless, and the gold loop attached to it had been threaded onto the delicate red ribbon that had formed the bow.

Now she lifted the ends of the ribbon while Lin held the paper scene.

Putting the paper on the table beneath the potted Christmas tree, Lin asked, "You like?"

"Oh, Lin, I love it. It's-it's—" The tears she had been holding back spilled over and she could not speak.

In her quiet, noble way Lin took charge so Violet might regain her emotions. She took the necklace, motioned for Violet to turn around, and tied the ribbons together at the back of her neck. She adjusted the loops on the bow she created before moving to stand in front of Violet and declare, "It is perfect."

Violet wrapped her arm around the other woman. Words were not adequate, so she hoped her feelings were conveyed with the sisterly embrace.

"Thank you, Lin. So very much."

"You are welcome."

Violet fingered the delicate pearl. It felt old, almost ancient.

"It is from China, isn't it?"

"From grandmother. Who got it from her grandmother. And maybe another grandmother, I do not know. It passed through family. And now, it passes through family again."

Chapter 44

It felt as if every family in Wylder had come out for the Christmas party.

Buckboards and buggies of all sizes were parked on the back street, Old Cheyenne Road, and the end of Wylder Road nearest the school. Corrals and stalls in and near the livery were full. Carriages, both plain and fancy, angled beside each other against snowbanks.

Horses were tied to hitching posts. One had its reins dangling in the wishing well. Some wore feed bags while others nickered in the cold evening air.

Conversation and laughter filled the schoolhouse. Folks who saw each other at weddings, funerals, or community get-togethers like this one had a lot to say—and a few hours in which to say it all.

Everyone who walked into the schoolroom complimented Violet on her teaching success. The community seemed pleased to have her, and that was a mighty big blessing.

Lin remained by her side. Violet introduced her as a dear friend from South Carolina, and no one seemed to suspect the untruth. They had discussed the falsehood with Sheriff Hanson beforehand. He agreed it best if Wylder's citizens did not know that a princess resided among them. It would be a shame if word got out and prevented Lin from living a peaceful life in town. She deserved some calm after the storms she had weathered, and giving her a cover story would get her that.

Mister Lui arrived at the party and, after hanging his jacket and hat on the pegs beside the door, made a beeline for Lin and Violet. He came with a smile on his face and a gift in his hands, which he handed to Violet with a tiny bow.

"For the wise teacher. I hope you heal easily and that when you no longer require an arm bandage you would use this as a shawl or for another useful purpose."

Violet was wearing the dragon print wrap that he had wound around her broken arm when she fell. It had enough red in it that it coordinated with her red holiday dress. The piece of fabric he gifted her now featured a green background with yellow lotus flowers embroidered onto it.

"Mister Lui, this is gorgeous. Thank you so much—you really are too kind."

He smiled at her display of pleasure. "In Chinese culture, the lotus is a very meaningful flower. It can grow from mud and make exquisite blooms. It does not need an ornate garden to bring beauty to life." The gentleman turned a palm up and swept it to the crowded room. "Yellow is the color of enlightenment so the fabric tells the story of one who brings wisdom and blooms beautifully wherever planted. You are our lotus blossom, Miss Bloom."

Violet's mouth opened but she didn't have words to put to her feelings. Mister Lui knowingly nodded, smiled, and turned to Lin.

He reached into his jacket pocket and pulled out a rectangular velvet box. "This is a token of my affection.

I hope you will wear it and think fondly of a man who is pleased to meet the magical Chinese woman who accompanies him in his dreams of home."

The box contained a bracelet. A row of black pearls adorned a gold chain. Watching him fasten it onto Lin's delicate wrist, Violet thought that it must be very precious.

But when the Chinese pair spoke softly in their native tongue, she saw the truth. They were precious, together.

Violet had heard of love at first sight, but until this very moment she had not believed it possible. Watching Lin and Mister Lui, she saw that she had been mistaken. It was possible—and very touching to witness.

Pulling herself from the scene, she turned to the room and looked for her pupils. She had instructed them to be near the singing platforms at precisely seven o'clock. They were there, waiting for her with expectant smiles on their cheerful faces.

They all knew that after their singing presentation Santa might visit the schoolroom.

And after that, there would be food and gifts for all.

Violet walked over to the children. They were so eager to show off for their families that some of their cheeks were apple red. A few were nervous so she patted a couple of shoulders and murmured words of encouragement. Then she directed them into place, with the taller children in the back row and the younger, smaller ones in front.

She smiled at Alexia, who returned the gesture. The girl stood shoulder to shoulder with her new best friend, Brenda. They both wore dark green dresses and looked like sisters.

Violet had learned that Alexia's mother and younger brother died during an influenza outbreak the previous winter. Her grieving father had sold their homestead to his brother and bought a home in town. Then he sent his daughter to stay with family back east when he became too devastated to care for her.

It had been nearly a year since the tragedy, and both were on their way to healing. The fact that Alexia had come home, remained with her father, and now they were beaming, represented a huge step forward for them.

A little Christmas miracle.

She looked at Beatie Milligan who stood in the center of the bottom row. Violet had been wondering if the child would consent to sing with the others. It pleased her to see her pupil apparently had a change of heart. She winked at the little girl and got a fast wave in return.

Violet turned to face the assemblage and clapped her left hand on the nearest bench. When the merriment died down and she had everyone's attention, she took a big leap of faith and began her speech to the residents of Wylder. Her tummy had a herd of reindeer dancing in it, but fortunately none of the jolly faces in front of her could see that.

"Welcome, everyone. Welcome to our Christmas program. This is the first year I have had the honor to serve the community as your schoolteacher, so I want to take a moment to thank you for giving me this opportunity. You've made me feel welcome in this wonderful town. You've given me a new home, a sense of purpose, and you have shared your children with me.

You are all, for me, a Christmas blessing. Thank you."

The applause that followed her small speech made her nearly overcome with emotion. When she looked out into the crowd at the familiar faces, she finally felt as if she truly belonged in Wylder.

Thomas stood to one side. He smiled at her and nodded when their gazes met. Beside him, a man who bore such a close resemblance that he had to be the uncle Alexia had mentioned. And near them both, their sister.

"The children have a short program prepared for all of you. They have practiced so I know you will be pleased by how beautifully they sing."

She turned her back on the crowd and faced the children. They had rehearsed the program in its entirety yesterday so she felt confident there would be no surprises or off-key renditions now. Violet raised a hand to prompt them, and they began to sing.

"Silent Night" went off without a hitch. Every child hit every note at the right time, and they were so inspiring that as the last "heavenly peace" died out the crowd drew in a collective breath.

She had planned to go right into the next song but Wylder's citizenry had different ideas. They clapped so long and hard that the children all giggled. Some hid behind their hands and laughed while others applauded for themselves.

Eventually, the room quieted enough for her to address the crowd. "The children have another song for you that we know will get you in the Christmas spirit." She had placed the leather straps with the sleigh bells on a nearby bench but before she could grab them and hand them out, Beatie Milligan took a giant step forward, out of the line.

Violet attempted to get the girl's attention, but the child would not look at her. Instead, she stared into the group and said in a clear voice, "And unto them a child was born. And it was Christmas."

A hush fell over the crowd. The children were quiet. The adults did not move. There were no feet shuffling, no hands rubbing together for warmth, and no whispers. There wasn't even a popping sound from the roaring fire in the belly stove.

The schoolroom went silent.

Beatie began to sing. "Rock-a-bye, Jesus, on the tree top…"

At "when the wind blows" the rest of the children joined in.

By the time they reached what should have been the final "cradle and all" the adults were singing—and they started the song from the beginning again.

Beatie wore a face-splitting grin. The children were all smiling, too. And parents, friends, and townsfolk had their arms about each other and were singing as if this were an actual birthday party for the baby Jesus.

Violet sang, too, and when she caught Beatie's attention she gave her a huge smile that she hoped conveyed as much love and joy as the little girl had bestowed upon the crowd. As they reached the final lines of the second round, Violet handed out the jingle bells. When she held a strap out to Beatie, the child took it and began to jangle.

Everyone agreed that there had never been a jinglier rendition of "Jingle Bells" in the entire Wyoming territory—or a better Christmas program.

When the singing ended and Santa arrived, some

folks went to the refreshment tables while their children were occupied by the jolly-yet-somewhat-familiar figure in the red suit.

Santa sat on his throne, handed out stockings, and ho-ho-hoed until every child had been convinced they'd met the man who drove a team of reindeer. There were so many smiles that they outshone the candles on the tree and were even more plentiful than the extra mints that sat in buckets around the room, courtesy of Finn at the Wylder Mercantile.

Violet made her way over to Thomas. She hadn't met his brother yet, and it seemed important to do so.

"Welcome to the schoolroom. I'm Violet Bloom, the teacher here. I'm sorry but I don't believe we've met yet." Mother had been such a stickler about her daughters feeling comfortable with new acquaintances that Violet felt no trepidation as she addressed the newcomer.

"I'm sorry, I haven't had a chance to introduce my brother." The crowd brought them so close she caught a whiff of the tobacco Thomas favored. "Miss Bloom, Mister Theodore Harvey. My brother now owns the homestead that my wife and I undertook when we came out west. We lived there until last year. Then I sold my holdings to Theo and moved into town."

"It's a pleasure to make your acquaintance, Miss Bloom. I've heard a great deal about you." Theodore Harvey's mannerisms were like his brother's, but he had a bit less polish. The man's hands bore signs of hard work and the muscles rippling beneath his jacket looked substantial. But he had a gentle tone and a sense of humor. "Tom's right. I live out at the homestead, all by my lonesome. You wouldn't by any chance have an unmarried sister, would you?"

She laughed. "As a matter of fact, I have three. Lily, the eldest, then Daisy, and finally, Pansy."

He wore a beard that he now stroked with a thoughtful air. "Hmm...I've always been kind of partial to lilies..."

They chatted for a few minutes before she had to excuse herself to see to the other guests. Violet made a point to visit with each family. And when they began to leave, she saw to it that they all took something home with them. There were decorations in abundance, and she wanted every home to have a remembrance from this special night.

Lin and Mister Liu did not leave each other at all during the party. Violet watched as the pair laughed, ate, and talked all evening long. The past had been harsh for the princess, but it appeared that her present, and perhaps her future, would be less arduous.

Thomas walked over to where she stood beside the Christmas tree. "Well, it seems as if you've put on the greatest event of the century. We'll be talking about this evening well into next year, if the comments I've heard from everyone are true—which they are. We have had a wonderful time. Thank you for caring enough to put your heart into this. I know I speak for everyone when I say we are grateful."

"You're very kind. I want everyone to have fun. We all deserve it, don't we?"

He looked down at her with an amused expression. His lips twitched and she stared at them, almost bewitched by the sight and nearness of the man. She remembered how his lips felt on hers, and how his kiss made her feel things she had never even dreamed of.

"We do, indeed." He lowered his voice and leaned close enough to whisper in her ear. "I do believe that if I were to tell you how much fun I want to have with you, you might give me a Christmas slap across the face." He straightened and met her gaze squarely. "But I assure you, it would be worth the slap."

Her heartbeat quickened. "Why, how on earth would it be worth a slap?"

He shrugged. "Feeling your hand on my face would make it worth it."

Violet raised both eyebrows and clamped her lips closed, not at all certain how to reply.

"Don't worry, Miss Bloom, I won't do anything to get myself thrown out of your schoolroom." Suddenly, he stopped teasing, almost as if he had run into a mental barrier. When he spoke, his voice lost the playful tone and turned serious. "Honestly, I'm not ready to do any of that, and I think you should know it. I admit, I'm starting to feel like laughing again, like I'm still alive, and I'm even thinking I might be able to spend time with someone special."

When he stopped, she did not press him to go on.

Silence often says all that needs to be said, so Violet waited a bit. Then she reached a hand out and pressed his upper arm gently. "I understand. Really, I do."

"Thank you. I want you to know that this time we've spent together has shown me that I didn't die last year. I thought for sure I had."

"I'm glad you were wrong."

"Me, too." He chuckled before he turned serious again. "Look, I know how you feel about northern men and I don't blame you one bit. You probably witnessed a lot and lost a lot more. We're all devils to you, I know that. But I want to say—"

Violet put a finger across his lips. It was bound to cause some folks to gossip but she didn't care.

She pulled her hand away, stuck it in her skirt pocket so she wouldn't be tempted to touch him again, and said, "People change. My beliefs were wrong. I see that now, and I'm sorry. Let's call it a Christmas miracle, this situation where two people find peace after chaos."

He shook his head, as if to clear it. "Are you saying you'll consider keeping company with me—and taking things nice and slow—now?"

"I am. And I will, gladly."

Thomas pulled a velvet-wrapped package from his inside jacket pocket and handed it to her. "Merry Christmas."

She recognized the green-and-red plaid bow fabric. "You're the one who delivered the Christmas tree to my house."

"Every house should have a tree. Are you going to open that?"

Inside the box a pair of gold earrings lay on a bed of red velvet. They were simple and classic—and resembled a pair her mother had given her when she graduated from teacher's college.

"They are beautiful. Thank you."

"I noticed you were missing an earring the morning you landed in that snowbank. When we got to my house, you were wearing only one. I assumed it must have fallen off when you fell so I went back to look, but I didn't find it. I hope these please you—they reminded me of you the minute I saw them. Some things are so lovely they take a man's breath away."

Violet wondered how slow they were going to have to take this keeping company arrangement. Right now, she could have thrown herself into his arms and kissed him until his head spun.

Instead, she smiled and said, "I love them. Thank you."

Chapter 45

Violet and Lin didn't want to return to the schoolhouse on Christmas Day to tidy up, so they remained after the guests went home. Once the last buckboard rumbled off into the distance, they began gathering up pinecone ornaments and mints from the tables.

Tate and Mister Liu stayed long enough to take the garlands down. They would have remained, but the women assured them that they were fine.

Sheriff Hanson, changed from his red velvet suit back into his usual attire, congratulated them on giving the town a fabulous holiday to remember.

He raised his voice as he looked around the empty schoolroom. "Well, it looks as if you're almost done here. If you're sure you don't need any help, I'll head on home now."

Violet waved him toward the door. "Nothing to worry about, Sheriff. We don't mind being here alone. Why, it's nearly Christmas! We'll finish clearing up and start home ourselves."

"That sounds like a plan. Remember to lock up, ladies. And Merry Christmas."

The sheriff tipped his black hat as he turned and headed out the door.

When it shut behind him, the big room fell eerily quiet.

Lin and Violet had discussed this plan with Sheriff Hanson before the party. They decided that if the Chinese villains did not make a move during the festivities, they might be coaxed into a false sense of security and show themselves afterward. The key enticement, to give the impression that the women were alone and defenseless, had gone off without a hitch.

Violet looked at Lin.

Lin's eyes held a steely glint in their deep brown depths.

They continued to chatter as if they were confident that they were safe.

The desks and benches were straightened out, the floor swept, and the chalkboard wiped and washed. The children had a holiday recess that lasted until next Monday, so Violet did not attempt to write a new daily message on the board. Perhaps by next week, her arm would be greatly improved.

Finally, there wasn't one thing out of place and the schoolroom sparkled. Even the Christmas tree had been so well watered it looked as if it were growing inside its bucket.

Violet and Lin stood back and admired their handiwork. The complete stillness was so profound, it almost seemed impossible that a few short hours ago the building been filled with loud laughter and exuberant singing.

She put her left arm around Lin's shoulders. "Well, I guess we're finished here. Thank you for helping me get the place cleaned up. I couldn't have done it without you."

Lin stifled a yawn with the back of one hand. "Family works together."

"You're right. Now, let's work on getting home. I believe we shall stay in bed later than usual tomorrow morning and observe the holiday in our nightclothes. I, for one, am exhausted."

"I, too."

They got their coats, hats, gloves, and scarves and dressed for the short, snowy walk.

Lin banked down the fire while Violet checked the candles on the tree once more. They were all out and their wicks were cold and blackened. They were safe to leave.

Violet blew out the last lamp on her desk while Lin grabbed the oil lamp used for travel.

They went to the front door and paused to take one last look around.

Lin's soft soprano broke the silence. "Silent night, holy night. All is calm, all is bright…"

Linking arms, they went outdoors.

Feathery flakes fell from the sky, landing on their heads so softly they felt like the brush of angels' wings.

Lin tilted her face and opened her mouth. She closed her eyes and waited for the snowflakes to fall on her tongue.

She opened one eye and gazed at Violet. Arching one perfectly shaped brow, she waited for Violet to tilt her head back and open her own mouth.

They stood catching snowflakes on their tongues for a few minutes. The air was still, and the temperature hadn't dipped low.

"We should get home, Lin."

The other nodded. "Yes. Let us go home."

Snow crunched underfoot as they walked across the schoolyard.

"Tomorrow I will have to write many notes to those who donated their time and talents so graciously to our celebration. People like Tate and Missus Milligan. Also, Gertie, who I must ask for the recipe for her special pumpkin bread. I don't recall when I've had a tastier bread."

Lin stopped walking. "She baked one for us—for Christmas breakfast. It is in the schoolroom."

"Well, we can't leave it for the mice to eat, can we? Besides, it will be a wonderful start to our day. What a kind woman! See? I really must write some thank you notes tomorrow."

They were a short way from the front door, so they turned and went back.

Lin entered, held the lamp high, and walked straight over to the Christmas tree. She picked up the wrapped pumpkin bread and waved it in the air. "I have it!"

Violet opened her mouth to reply, but before she could utter a word a dark shape emerged from behind the wood stove. It moved so fast that it appeared to cross the room in less time than it takes for a heart to beat.

"Lin! Watch out!"

The figure grabbed her friend from behind and lifted her right off her feet. Lin kicked out and wrenched from side to side. She screamed in Chinese which made the man loosen his grip for an instant.

She took that opening and swung her arm around to hit him in the face. Pumpkin bread didn't make the best weapon, so it did not deter the man. As the loaf crumbled onto the floor, he swung Lin's body in a circle, yelling in Chinese as he tossed her about like a puppet.

The lantern crashed onto the floor. Oil spread on the floorboards and blue flames licked their way across the space.

Violet ran to help Lin but a force from behind knocked her off her feet. She fell onto her injured arm. As white-hot surges of pain spiraled toward her center, the figure that pushed her down climbed on top of her.

Anger and hatred shone in his eyes. She saw that he meant to kill her.

Dark ink wound out from beneath the hair at his right temple, down his cheek, and onto his chin. Disgust mixed with fear as she struggled to get away from the man with the snake tattooed on his face.

Lin's cries for help mingled with the sound of popping noises.

Violet remembered the gun in her pocket, so she wrestled her arm down to her hip. Her assailant smirked and said something in Chinese that sounded cruel. Then he reached between them and pushed her skirts high, and she understood his intentions.

Her hand floundered in the fabric bunched up over her knees, but she persisted, searching for the weapon that might save them.

She found her pocket and pushed her hand inside, even as the man's palm touched the delicate skin on her inner thigh. Violet fought revulsion. She choked on the smoke that began to fill her lungs.

Her fingers found the derringer, so she angled the pocket upward, toward the despicable human who had placed his hand where it wasn't invited. She pulled the trigger.

The sound was deafening.

She gagged when his hand dropped at the apex of her thighs and his body crumpled on top of hers. His head fell forward onto her shoulder, bringing the ugly tattoo inches from her eyes.

Violet screamed.

She pushed at his shoulders and twisted beneath the dead man, but her skirts were tangled around her legs. She kicked at him and pushed again—and suddenly his body was torn from hers.

Powerful arms lifted her and carried her from the smoky room. She resisted, trying to find release so she could help the woman who had become as beloved to her as her other sisters were.

"Lin! They have Lin!"

Thomas crushed her against him. "No—Wei has Lin. She's in safe hands."

The move from stifling heat to chilled air brought on a fit of coughing. Thomas carried her away from the schoolhouse, put her on her feet, and held her as she gasped for air.

When she could speak, she met his gaze and asked, "Lin? Please, tell me she is unhurt!"

He took her by the shoulders and turned her so she could see the couple standing beneath an oak tree that grew between the schoolhouse and the rectory. Lin and Mister Liu were in each other's arms and both appeared fine.

Violet looked up into Thomas's deep brown eyes. In the darkness she recognized the truth in them. It required no effort because it was the truth of her own heartbeat, too.

"Thank you for saving me again."

"I'm sorry it took so long. We figured they would

be waiting at your house, so we were there. Except Wei—he would not go that far from his princess—and those were his exact words. He calls her his princess."

She did not comment on that. It would be up to Lin—and Wei, also—to keep or share the meaning of the endearment.

"But you got here so quickly. It felt like the attack happened in a heartbeat, Thomas. It was so fast—and horrible!" She covered her face in her hand and shuddered.

He pulled her close. "We heard the shots."

She looked up at him. "Shots? But I only fired once."

"Wei shot to sound the alarm."

Those were the sounds she heard inside the schoolhouse while they were scuffling with the assassins. It made sense now.

"I heard them. Thank goodness he stayed behind."

"Because of Wei's quick thinking, we'll be able to save the schoolhouse, too."

They turned to face the building. Flames were being extinguished by what seemed like most of the men in Wylder. They passed buckets of water and snow from man to man, into the front door and onto the fire.

"The Chinese men?"

"They won't bother anyone again. You took care of the snake-faced bastard and Earl has the other one tied to a tree over yonder. Let's just say he won't be able to walk to his hangin'. Pretty sure his legs were broken during his rescue from the fire."

Violet didn't feel one ounce of remorse for killing a man. And she didn't feel sorry for the man with the broken legs, either. She planned to be standing in the front row when he got his due.

In a heartbeat, she had nearly lost all that she held dear.

And in another heartbeat, it had all been returned.

Violet knew she must look frightful, but she did not care. She met Thomas's gaze. "I have to ask you a question and I want you to give me your sincere reply, please."

"I promise I will forevermore be completely honest with you. You have my word. What is it you need to know on this wild Christmas Eve?"

"Thomas, how slowly do you intend to court me?"

The corner of his upper lip lifted as he shook his head. "Not very slowly at all. In fact, I think that we need to move our courtship along, enjoy every minute we have together, and love as passionately as anyone ever has."

She quirked an eyebrow. "Passion...I must admit, I'm not as skilled in certain areas as I believe you might be. Remember, Wylder's schoolteacher is an unmarried lady..."

He growled as his lips claimed hers. The kiss was tender, loving, and filled with promises of what lay ahead.

When he released her mouth, Thomas put a cheek against hers. "It will be my pleasure to teach the teacher, although I have to admit she has already taught me plenty."

"Then we shall both be pupils." Her heart was full as she settled into the circle of his arms. She had found her way home. "It must be past midnight by now, don't you think?"

"I believe you're right." He leaned in to kiss her

again. Before his lips touched hers, Thomas murmured, "Merry Wylder Christmas, Violet."

A word about the author...

Sarita Leone loves happy endings—in life and on the page.

When she's not busy writing her next novel, this adventure-loving yoga teacher likes to hike, travel, and dance beneath the stars. She studies languages, enjoys making a mess in the kitchen, and never says "no" to fun. Finding pockets of peace everywhere she goes, this author plans to make every moment of this journey count.